HOW
to hide an
ALIEN

For Otis, George, Eddie and William

STRIPES PUBLISHING LIMITED

An imprint of the Little Tiger Group
1 Coda Studios, 189 Munster Road, London SW6 6AW

Imported into the EEA by Penguin Random House Ireland,
Morrison Chambers, 32 Nassau Street, Dublin D02 YH68

A paperback original
First published in Great Britain in 2022

Text copyright © Karen McCombie, 2022
Illustration copyright © Thy Bui, 2022

ISBN: 978-1-78895-110-4

A CIP catalogue record for this book is available
from the British Library.

Printed and bound in the UK.

The Forest Stewardship Council® (FSC®) is a global, not-for-profit
organization dedicated to the promotion of responsible forest
management worldwide. FSC defines standards based on agreed
principles for responsible forest stewardship that are supported by
environmental, social, and economic stakeholders. To learn more,
visit www.fsc.org

MIX
Paper from
responsible sources
FSC
www.fsc.org   FSC® C171272

2 4 6 8 10 9 7 5 3 1

How to hide an Alien

KAREN McCOMBIE

LITTLE TIGER
LONDON

The best kept secret in town

The people of Fairfield hadn't a clue.

After the wild and sudden storms of the last few weeks, they were glad that everything seemed *just* about back to being boringly normal.

And, as far as they were concerned, today was an ordinary, sleepy Sunday. In the autumn-leaved park, parents chatted as their children played. Naturally, they discussed the freak lightning bolt that had recently struck the local secondary school during its Open Evening, but then their conversation drifted to plans for outings to the annual funfair that would be setting up in the park any day now.

Down by the River Wouze, teenagers slouched on the railings and gawped at the shattered windows of Riverside Academy and the huge, hazard-taped crater in the playground. Passing gum around, they discussed going to see the new blockbuster movie the following day, since school would still be closed (yay!).

Wherever they were and whatever they were doing, the entire population of Fairfield would have been shocked – or more likely *petrified* – if they'd known what was going on right under their noses. Or up at the shabby parade of shops on Hill Street, on the north side of town, to be precise.

Between the ordinary-looking laundrette and the faded grocer's, the Electrical Emporium repair shop practically *glowed* with the secret stashed in its back room. Ever since Thursday's supposed 'lightning strike', this unremarkable spot had become a safe haven for a very special visitor.

A homeless alien. A Star Boy stranded far, far from his solar system...

But there *was* one thing that the unwitting residents of Fairfield had in common with the stowed-away Star Boy. *None* of them – human or otherwise – had the faintest inkling about the urgent mission being planned on an unimaginably distant planet. A mission to rescue the lost alien – who didn't *technically* want to be found.

Or that the spacecraft and its crew were scheduled to arrive around teatime next Thursday.

Sunday: A home far from home?

STAR BOY: A glimpse of the past

The back room of the Electrical Emporium was a messy muddle of things: a workspace where the temperamental kettles, toasters and PlayStations of Fairfield were fixed; a cosy living room with reams of semi-working fairy lights looped and dangling across every wall; a kitchen with a gurgling fridge and a sink full of often forgotten dishes.

And now it also contained an amber-coloured alien, who was currently scrolling through the data lens he wore in his left eye.

"Eight hundred and fifty-three thousand and two hundred seconds," the Star Boy announced in the English of this particular Earth region. He sat, crouched and glowing, on a moth-eaten rug, staring at the four Humans seated around him: the tall girl (Kiki), the short boy (Wes), the child (Ty) and the young man (Eddie).

"What are you on about?" asked his friend – and rescuer – Kiki.

"I fell to Earth eight hundred and fifty-three thousand and two hundred seconds ago," explained the Star Boy happily.

"You mean *ten days ago* you crash-landed in our school playground," suggested Wes, his other friend and rescuer. "That's how people would say it."

"Ah, yes, I understand," murmured the Star Boy.

He found the dazzling array of Human descriptions for time both baffling and fascinating. It could be talked about as seconds or minutes or hours. Days and nights could be split into categories such as 'dawn' and 'dusk' and 'lunchtime'.

"And you've been here at mine for three days," said Eddie, the owner of the Electrical Emporium and repairer of broken things.

Eddie had been most kind. After the destruction of the Star Boy's school-basement refuge, Eddie had given him shelter here. And, not only that, he'd dragged a small generator into the higgledy-piggledy back room, so that the energy-depleted alien could recharge.

All the Star Boy's rescuers had been so very welcoming. The Star Boy suddenly wished he could do something for them in return, but what? And then it occurred to him that, during discussions and comparisons of their respective worlds, he had not been able to adequately describe what his everyday environment looked like, as its constant electrical brightness was so unlike anything found on Earth. But, with his gaze falling on to the black rectangle of the TV box, the Star Boy wondered if he could transmute images of his home planet on to the screen.

"Please may I have your attention?" the Star Boy requested of his friends. "I would like you all to watch this..."

Ty bounced on the sofa beside Kiki. "What's happening? Are you going to show us your alien SUPERPOWER?" he asked excitedly.

Kiki shushed her brother as the Star Boy turned and stared intently at the TV that was balanced on top of the generator.

"What exactly are you trying to do, Stan?" he

heard Kiki ask, using the Human name they'd settled on calling him. The Star Boy liked it. He felt happy to be known as Stan – Stan Boyd, in fact. All of his life so far, the Star Boy had simply been referred to as a long line of unmemorable code.

"I am attempting to download visual information from my data lens on to this primitive machine," he explained, his intense concentration causing crackles to ignite inside and across his chest.

"What sort of visual information? What are you going to show us, Stan?" Wes asked next.

"My home," said the Star Boy.

Home: the place where someone lives. That was no longer true for Stan.

His home was lost to him, gone. He'd never return. And the Star Boy was glad of it.

When the Others had arrived – under cover of rumbling storm clouds and darkness – and lasered his stricken craft to ashes, it had been terrifying. His former classmates had presumed him already dead, and in this final act they hoped to hide all evidence of his existence – but their actions had set him free.

Free to experience something no other Star Boy ever had. Free to interact with members of a completely alien species. Which included Kiki and Wes, Ty and Eddie.

Already he felt more of a kinship with this mismatched collection of Humans than with anyone back on his planet, where the concept of having 'friends' and 'family' was completely unfamiliar.

"Your home...? You mean you're going to show us your old HOUSE?" Ty asked.

"Ty, Stan already told us there are no houses where he's from," Kiki reminded her little brother.

"Yeah, children grow up in Education Zones," Wes added.

"And adults live in Work Zones, is that right?" asked Eddie, glancing around.

"YES! That's RIGHT!" barked Ty. "Kids don't EVER know their mums and dads and brothers and sisters. That would make me SO sad! Does it make YOU so sad, Stan?"

The Star Boy was too focused to respond. He had just sourced the perfect piece of imagery to show them: the occasion when the Absolute graciously visited his particular Education Zone.

"Observe..." he muttered, lifting his spindly arm and pointing the thumb of his fin-shaped hand towards the darkened glass screen.

As the familiar scene began to emerge, a word suddenly came to the Star Boy's lips: the name of his planet. He was taken aback to find that the very sound of it, the *saying* of the word, caused a deep ache to radiate across his chest.

Was it possible to be glad and sad at the same time?

Emotions were discouraged among his species. And he had certainly never experienced two opposing emotions at once. Was this a Human trait? He'd have to ask his new friends. He knew he'd have many, many questions for them in the coming days and weeks – and months and years! – as he settled into his new life in the town of Fairfield, Earth.

WES: Seeing into space – sort of

Wes exchanged a quick grin of excitement with Kiki over the top of her brother's head. What they were all about to see would be an awesome first for humankind. A real-life glimpse of a real-life alien planet...

How many scientists, astronomers and world leaders would give ANYTHING to be in my shoes right now? thought Wes. In the size seven trainers of an ordinary twelve-year-old schoolboy?

He turned back to face the TV, his heart beating harder, faster as he noticed something beginning to form on the blackened screen. Pinpricks of dancing white pixels fizzing through the darkness.

"When's it going to START?" asked Ty, his loud whisper startling Wes.

"Shh ... any second," Wes assured him, as he waited for the flickering, blindingly white interference on the screen to transform into an alien scene.

"Well, it's a bit BORING so far," Ty grumbled, as he wriggled and squiggled between Wes and Kiki like a fidgety frog.

"Ty! Don't be rude!" Kiki shushed him.

"But nothing's happening, IS it?" Ty continued bluntly. "Can we go and see if the FUNFAIR'S arrived in the park?"

"Ty, be cool. Stan's concentrating," said Eddie, who regularly looked after Ty and was well used to his bounciness.

"But Stan will LOVE the funfair!" Ty protested. "It's TOTALLY brilliant. It only comes to town once a year, Stan, and there are TONS of rides. I could take you on the ghost train!"

The Star Boy was concentrating so hard on his efforts that he didn't react to Ty's offer, Wes noted.

"That's a great idea, Ty, but the funfair doesn't open till Wednesday, does it?" Wes heard Kiki wearily remind her brother.

"And what we're about to see is going to be a

million, *zillion* times better than any funfair ride!" said Wes, even though he'd never, ever been to a funfair, so could hardly comment. "Just give it a minute or two..."

The Star Boy suddenly swivelled round to face them all, his inky-black eyes blink-blinking from side to side, his slitted nostrils fluttering.

"Give it a minute or two? But ... but it is already *there*!" he said animatedly, waving his thumbed fin at the TV behind him. "You cannot see the main thoroughfare by the Education Zone?"

"Huh?" grunted Ty.

"I think Stan means the road outside his school," Wes translated, though he couldn't see anything beyond the quivering static. Like Kiki and Eddie, Wes leaned forward, peering at the TV, searching for anything in the fractured nothing...

"And there are the crowds of Star Boys, waiting to welcome the Absolute!" the Star Boy tried again, pointing madly.

"The absolute what?" asked Wes.

"The Absolute is ... our leader, our guide, all-knowing!" the Star Boy replied, trying to convey who this VIP was. "It was a great honour that the

Absolute came to our zone, to meet the Masters and Star Boys and observe the work that we do."

Wes watched as Stan turned back to the TV, tilting his head to one side, enraptured by what he – and sadly he alone – could see.

"He sounds awesome, Stan, but we can't make him out!" Wes told the Star Boy, disappointment dragging at his chest.

"*Her!* The Absolute is of female origin!" the Star Boy said indignantly.

"OK, we can't make *her* out, or, well … any of what you're trying to show us," Wes continued, attempting a half-smile to soften the blow. "I'm sorry, but we can't seem to see things the way you can."

The Star Boy's glowing shoulders slumped in disappointment. Just as he'd struggled to translate the name of his home into a vaguely comprehensible Human term, it seemed that the images he was streaming couldn't shape themselves into anything a Human brain could process.

"I wanted very much to show you—" The Star Boy made the breathy sound that was the barely there name of his planet, but it was drowned out by a sudden shrill noise.

RING-RING! RING-RING!

"It's my dad – that's his FaceTime alert," Kiki said hurriedly, digging her hand into the back pocket of her jeans.

The old-fashioned ringtone was super loud. MUCH louder than it should have been coming from Kiki's pocket. And the reason, Wes realized, was because the screen of Kiki's phone was now visible on the TV, replacing the pixels that wouldn't unjumble.

"Kiki!" said Wes urgently.

A man with a beaming smile – presumably Kiki's dad – was looking straight at them, even before Kiki had retrieved her phone, even without her accepting the call.

"Hello? Kiki? Ty?" he said.

Wes sat statue-still in shock, same as everyone else in Eddie's back room.

Maybe Kiki's dad will think the screen is frozen and hang up, he thought hopefully and uselessly.

KIKI: The wriggly surprise

"Kiki? I can't see you properly, honey," said Dad, the sky blue of his kitchen walls visible behind him. "Something's blocking my view ... something fuzzy and orange. Have you got your finger over the camera?"

Kiki's eyes shot to the Star Boy, who was clearly the fuzzy orange something. Luckily, he'd realized that too and had flopped down on to the floor, just out of sight.

"Yeah ... sorry," said Kiki, pulling her phone from her pocket and waving it about. Which was a mistake, obviously.

"Wait – if THAT'S your mobile, what are you using for this call?" Dad asked, frowning from the TV.

"Hello, Mr Hamilton!" Eddie called out. "We're,

er, watching you on Kiki's iPad! It's been glitching, so Kiki brought it over for me to take a look..."

Until last Thursday, Kiki hadn't thought much of Eddie. He was just the young geeky bloke who ran the repair shop across the road. Someone who helped Mum out by dropping off or picking up Ty from school on his rickety motorbike and sidecar. But, since the drama of last Thursday evening, when he'd saved all their lives, Kiki had done a massive turnaround in her thinking. Eddie had been a complete hero. He'd also accepted the reality of their alien friend without TOTALLY freaking out, which he had every right to do. And now he was proving to be a truly *excellent* liar in a crisis.

"*DADDDDD!*" yelled Ty, jumping off the sofa and running towards the TV screen, skilfully sidestepping the Star Boy where he lay faceplanted on the rug.

"Hey, Ty!" said Dad, beaming. "So, how are you guys?"

"Riverside Academy got BLOWN UP last week," Ty blurted out. "And so Kiki doesn't have to go to school and that's SO not fair!"

"Yes, I know about Kiki's school, Ty," Dad said with a smile, amused by Ty's usual drama. "So anyway, are you going to introduce me to your friend?"

"You can SEE *STAN*?!" Ty piped up, as he looked down at the sprawled alien. Only he wasn't there, Kiki noticed with relief. The Star Boy must have paused his pulses and turned himself invisible.

"WES! Dad's talking about WES, Ty!" Kiki quickly corrected her brother.

"Oh," mumbled Ty. "I thought you meant you could see the ALIEN that we—"

"So yeah, Dad! This is Wes!" Kiki firmly interrupted. She felt the sofa cushion next to her give way, as someone unseen settled themselves in the space Ty had just vacated. "We've started hanging out at school. Haven't we, Wes?"

Kiki fixed a grin on her face and hoped she sounded convincing. Thankfully, Wes played along and nodded.

Turning back to Dad, Kiki couldn't help noticing his slight frown. Ever since the start of term, Kiki had boasted about the cool friendship group she was in, and here she was introducing a totally *new* friend. Still, now wasn't exactly the time to explain about the big fallout with Lola, Zainab and Saffron.

"Well, nice to meet you, Wes!" said Dad, shaking

off his confusion. "Anyway, Kiki, Ty … I'm just calling with a bit of a surprise. I thought I'd come for a visit on Wednesday, since the funfair's in town."

"YAY!" yelped Ty, punching the air.

"That's great, Dad!" Kiki said, breaking into a smile. Since he'd moved to Birmingham, they didn't get to see him as much as they'd have liked.

"It was actually Tasmin's idea. When she mentioned it, I thought, yeah, let's do it!" Dad explained.

Kiki nodded. That was nice of Dad's girlfriend. Going to the funfair had always been a family tradition. They'd even gone the year before, not long after Dad had moved out, which was sort of sad, but kind of lovely too, like it was proof that Mum and Dad still cared about each other. This year, Kiki had supposed it wouldn't happen. She'd thought Dad might be too busy with his new life. But nope – he was coming! Dad, Mum, Kiki and Ty … they wouldn't miss out this year after all!

"Glad you're both pleased," Dad beamed. "I've been telling Tasmin about all the rides. She says no way are we getting her on any of the really big ones – she hasn't got a head for heights!"

Kiki had to concentrate very hard to keep the smile from slipping right off her face. She didn't mind going out for dinner with Dad's girlfriend whenever they were visiting him, but as for Tasmin inviting herself along to a family tradition...

"But that's not ALL of the surprise," said Dad with a just-you-wait twinkle in his eye. "Meet Coco! She'll be coming with us and she can't wait to meet you!"

Dad budged up on the bench he was sitting on, just as his girlfriend appeared beside him, all smiles and with a wriggly something in her arms.

A *puppy*? Kiki was barely aware of her jaw dropping. Dad and Tasmin had got themselves a puppy, after all the pleading for a dog Kiki and Ty had done over the years?

"YAP! YAP! YAP! YAP!" yelped the scruffy, wriggly black bundle of fur and fat, flappy paws.

Uh-oh, thought Kiki, as the ache of unfairness in her chest was replaced by a sudden flood of dread.

The invisible alien sitting next to her had limited knowledge of non-human Earth creatures. Besides the pigeons he'd befriended in the school playground, the only other animal he'd encountered was Ty's hamster, whose high-pitched squeaking had greatly alarmed the Star Boy. A yappity puppy was likely to be as shocking as walking into Mr Pickle's shop next door and finding a sabre-toothed tiger growling in the crisps aisle.

"AAAAAA-EEEEEEE!" screeched the invisible Stan, right on cue.

"What on earth was THAT?" Dad yelled, as the puppy turned into a furry blur, scrabbling to get away from the scary noise.

"Like I said, faulty iPad!" Eddie yelled, rushing over and switching off the TV.

As the screen blacked out, Kiki winced, gently peeling the invisible finned hand and thumb from her arm where the Star Boy had gripped it in sheer fear.

"It's OK, Stan," Kiki said to the terrified boy beside her, in her best calm and soothing voice.

Inside, Kiki was anything but calm because that close call with Dad had just woken her up to reality. Last week had been intense and crazy; this weekend – hanging out with the Star Boy at Eddie's – had been fascinating and fun. But it hadn't properly sunk in till right *now* that Stan was here for good. Like,

FOREVER. What was she going to do with him? How could she keep him safe?

It was just a tiny bit *completely* overwhelming. But at least Kiki wasn't alone in this.

"Wes," she said, leaning over to see her friend better as the re-Morphing Star Boy took up the space between them. "If Stan's going to pass for a real human and fit in, we have a LOT of work to do. Starting *now*."

Kiki's firm words were instantly followed by the buzz of an incoming text on her phone. She knew it would be Mum's promised five-minute warning that tea was nearly ready.

"Starting *tomorrow*," Kiki corrected herself, feeling her tummy rumble in spite of everything.

WES: The life-changing lunchtime

"It's SO NOT FAIR that Dad's got a dog!" Ty whined, leaning against his sister as they stood on the pavement outside the Electrical Emporium.

Wes was fascinated by the relationship between Kiki and Ty. Most of the time Kiki acted like Ty was more annoying than a wasp around an ice cream, but her arm was wrapped about his shoulders right now, hugging him to her side.

"I know, Ty... So, Wes, meet me here at ten a.m. tomorrow?" Kiki suggested. "And before you ask again, Ty, no you *can't* skip school and come too."

"Aw..." groaned her brother. "But I WANT to help train Stan!"

"You can help another time – Stan'll need lots of training!" Wes jumped in, before replying to Kiki.

"Could we make it a bit later, like midday? My dad might need me for stuff in the morning..."

Wes's dad always needed him for stuff. Right now, Wes had to go and collect their washing from the Busy Bubbles laundrette next door to Eddie's shop.

"OK, see you then," said Kiki, dragging her brother by the hand across the street to their flat, as Wes headed into the laundrette.

"Thanks, Mrs Crosby!" he called out to a lady who was zipping up a large, well-stuffed rucksack. "You didn't have to pack it for me."

"My pleasure, Wesley!" replied Mrs Crosby, smoothing down the front of her overall. "Oh, and I meant to tell you – I heard a couple of customers talking about a new alien film that's just opened at the cinema. Thought that might be right up your street!"

Wes smiled as Mrs Cosby passed him a toffee from the handful she always kept in the pocket of her overalls.

"Thanks," he said, grateful for both the sweet and the recommendation. "Yeah – *Through Alien Eyes*. I've heard about that."

Wes had seen ads for the movie on TV, and on the side of buses around town. Any other week, it would've been *all* that he could think of. But today the new blockbuster was about as interesting to Wes as the pile of socks and pants swishing around in the suds of the nearest machine.

"Well, if you do go and see it, you can give me your review next week!" Mrs Crosby joked.

"Yeah, definitely!" Wes promised, as he hoicked the heavy bag on to his shoulder and trundled out of the open door.

Outside on the pavement, the autumn wind bit hard, and with his free hand Wes yanked up the hood of his Puffa jacket, pulling the strings tight so the circle of black padded nylon framed his round face and cowlick of white-blond hair.

Passing the Electrical Emporium again, Wes ached to go straight back inside, instead of heading home to—

"Careful!" A gruff voice called out a warning, as Wes narrowly missed tripping over a stand of newspapers that Mr Pickle was tidying.

"Sorry," mumbled Wes, sidestepping out of the shopkeeper's way, but not before he spotted the headline slammed on the front page of the local paper:

LIGHTNING-STRIKE: DEVASTATION

In that second, Wes imagined shocking the shopkeeper with the news that the explosion in the school grounds last Thursday was actually caused by an alien attack, not some rogue lightning strike.

And what if I told him there was an alien hiding just through the wall from all his rows of ketchup and tins of peas? thought Wes, grinning to himself as he set off down Hill Street with his heavy load.

Arriving at the junction with the high street, Wes grinned even wider at the sight of the movie poster for *Through Alien Eyes* on the side of the bus shelter by the town hall. It was a pretty dramatic image: a close-up of a neon-green eyeball with the silhouette of a frightened human reflected in it, hands held up in fear.

"Yeah, *right!*" he said to himself, thinking how incredibly untrue-to-life it was.

But Wes's muttered words were drowned out by the grumble and roar of approaching traffic. He turned to see a procession of huge trucks lumbering towards him – every one of them laden with bizarrely bright and compacted fairground rides. Wes watched, spellbound, as they passed by. He'd never been to a proper fair before. Once, when his mum was still around, he'd visited the summer fête in the village where they used to live, but the most exciting thing there had been a bouncy castle.

After the cavalcade had gone, Wes crossed the road, heading for the river and the pedestrian bridge that would take him over the choppy water of the River Wouze to the south side of town. His mind was still on the funfair; he'd love to go but who with? Kiki would be with her family, of course. Maybe he could take Stan? They could be fairground newbies together! How cool would that be?

But, as hard as he tried to picture them having fun on the dodgems, the only image he could conjure was Kiki's frown from earlier, when she spoke about how much the Star Boy had to learn. She probably wouldn't think it was safe for him to be somewhere as public as a fair, especially without her...

But it's still a couple of days till then, Wes told himself. If we keep coaching Stan, maybe we'd trust him enough to fit in and be around crowds by then?

Lost in thought, Wes suddenly noticed he wasn't alone on the narrow bridge; a dad held a small girl in his arms – they were both looking towards the twisted metal fencing and zigzagging hazard tape on the far side of the riverside path.

"Look, Daddy – diggers!" said the little girl, pointing at the yellow vehicles parked beside a yawning crater in the lower playground of Riverside Academy.

Staring in the same direction, Wes noticed that the giant metal wheelie bins were on their sides, tossed about in the blast as if they were empty baked-bean cans. Every window at the back of the school building was framed with spiked shards of broken glass. And then there was the space where a circle of towering bushes had once been, with the Star Boy's damaged space pod hidden among them. The plant life, the pod … all reduced to nothing more than a dusting of ash, drifting and spinning away with every gust of wind.

"See that hole in the ground? That's where the big lightning bolt came down," the dad was explaining, as Wes shuffled awkwardly past them with his bulky bag of laundry. "There were lots of grown-ups and children visiting the school that evening, but luckily no one was hurt."

Yeah, though some of us were very nearly killed, thought Wes, remembering his relief when Eddie roared up on his motorbike, and how he, Kiki, Ty and the Star Boy all piled gratefully on board, seconds before the strike happened.

"You mustn't worry about storms, though," the dad continued. "They aren't usually as fierce as—"

"Daddy, can we have chips for tea?" the little girl interrupted, losing interest in the wrecked school playground.

Wes smiled to himself. To the average resident of Fairfield, the blast was caused by a freak of nature – a talking point for a few days at most. And then life went on: people visited the park, made plans to see the latest movie, thought about the fair coming to town, wanted chips for their tea.

But it was different for Wes. Ever since that lunchtime – that magical lunchtime when an alien boy from an unpronounceable planet materialized in front of him and Kiki in the music room at school – his life had changed for the better. It was as if the Star Boy's amber glow had lit up everything in Wes's world, a world that had felt grey-edged and dull up till now. How incredibly lucky he was!

Oof! Wes was suddenly tugged sharply from behind, his rucksack half dragged off his shoulder. He tumbled backwards on to the bag, scrabbling his hands and legs in the air, like a flipped-over tortoise.

Lifting his head, Wes caught sight of a boy on a bike laughing as he veered off. Harvey Wickes: Year Seven football team captain, super cool in his *own* opinion, first-class idiot in Wes's.

Wes hadn't seen him since the Open Evening at school, when the Star Boy – hiding in plain sight as a student – had projected images of Harvey and Kiki's ex-friend Lola on to the overhead screen for all to see, showing them both at their bullying best. Luckily for Harvey and Lola, the storm had arrived with perfect timing, diverting everyone's attention as the sudden thunder roared and raged at the windows of the hall.

Still, it was pretty obvious that Harvey hadn't learned any lessons at all, and wasn't planning on changing his obnoxious behaviour any time soon...

Wes twisted on to his side, but before he could

get up a text alert pinged on his mobile. Dad.

Going for a nap. Can you put the laundry away? And get yourself something for tea.

Wes's heart sank. Dad never left the flat these days. And if he wasn't hunched over his computer, trying to keep his business afloat, he was in bed, 'having a nap'. A nap that could last for hours.

Wes shivered in the chill of the wind as he got to his feet, heaved the bag back on to his shoulder and continued over the bridge in the direction of home.

Home. It was a cosy word for most people, Wes supposed. But to him home meant endless chores and a dad who seemed to be turning to stone.

"But hey, I'm lucky. I've got THE best secret in the world!" Wes whispered to himself, as he tried to ignore Harvey's casual shove and his dread of going back to the crushing loneliness of the flat.

Yet the glowing amber of the day seemed to seep away with every step. It dripped over the edges of the bridge and sank into the lapping browny-grey waves of the Wouze.

STAR BOY: The ping of a pang

"Night!" Eddie called out, as he went through the door that led to the rest of the building, which the Star Boy had not yet seen.

He didn't understand why Eddie had announced that it was night-time. But it was said in a friendly way, so he decided to try saying it back.

"Yes, it is night!" the Star Boy replied from his now-regular spot on the worn patterned rug, his back against the small generator, the electricity buzzing and sizzling into his system.

The only response the Star Boy heard was a snorting noise that sounded a little like a laugh that faded as Eddie ambled away.

Alone now, the Star Boy decided to use this resting period as he often did: to study.

Scrolling through data, he quickly sourced footage of young dogs. The Star Boy's aim was to acclimatize himself to the sudden sharp sounds and movements they made. He was keen to do this as he hoped Kiki would introduce him to the tiny canine owned by her father and the smiling woman on the video call, and the Star Boy didn't want to embarrass Kiki by responding inappropriately, i.e. screaming again.

Studying the world of pets in general absorbed him for some time. He found it peculiar that some animals were deemed suitable to be pets and some not. For example, budgies and fish small-as-a-thumbnail might be a pet, but slugs and ladybirds were not.

The subject was baffling.

Who wouldn't want to own something as spectacular and perfect as a ladybird? thought the Star Boy, as he stopped his data spooling and leaned away from the generator. His strength had now completely returned, he realized.

Oh, how wondrous it felt to be fully rebooted, and to know he could carry on exploring and experiencing the wonders of his new hometown of

Fairfield! Perhaps tomorrow he might try to Morph, to turn from Star Boy to Stan Boyd. He had very much enjoyed doing so last week: becoming Human, wearing the borrowed clothings of a student and wandering the corridors of Riverside Academy.

And hadn't the small Human Ty mentioned something he might enjoy? A vehicle called a 'ghostly train'?

Setting his data lens to source information about ghostly trains, the Star Boy didn't initially notice the fairy lights dipping and surging on the four walls around him.

Am I causing that? the Star Boy wondered to himself, as the colourful lights danced in random on-off patterns.

He held still, but couldn't sense any malfunctioning in his system. Yet he supposed he *might* be responsible for it, just as he *must* have been responsible for the glitch earlier, when Kiki's video message had appeared on the TV screen. Perhaps his electrical energy needed recalibrating after everything he'd been through?

Running a second assessment of his internal systems, it did appear that his temperature was running a little high. Might some coolness in the Outside help...?

The Star Boy got up, and walked over to the door in the back wall of the kitchen area. Just as he was about to turn the heavy key in the lock, he remembered to pause his pulses and let his three hearts stop, to allow his amber glow to fade to invisibility.

Safe now, the Star Boy turned first the key and then the cold-to-the-touch brass doorknob, and let himself out into the small, walled yard. Immediately, he dropped to the ground and stretched out on the uneven paving stones.

His senses quivered with pleasure. The chilly night air settled upon him like a weighted blanket. His nostrils fluttered at the scents of earth and dampness, of oil and metal and rust from the motorcycle parked close by.

Splaying his fin-shaped hands wide over the rough stones, the Star Boy closed his eyes and concentrated on the infinitesimal vibrations of life below the slabs, of worms and mites and other assorted insects going about their business in the dark earth.

He noted too the crinkle of barely there roots

extending and unfurling, fledgling plants ready to peek between the paving stones whenever the warmth of the sun drew them upwards.

Then, flicking his eyes open, he beheld the familiar inky darkness of the night sky, dotted with speckles of stars and planets. All so pretty but insignificant from here, all so intimidatingly vast when he was passing them by in his pod just a few night-times ago.

How strange to think he'd never travel in that startling and wondrous realm again, that this would forever be his view of what Humans called space! As the Star Boy stared, he was startled by a pinging sensation in the area of his chest. A fleeting, painful sort of ping, which Humans would call a 'pang', he supposed, running a check on his data lens.

• pang = a sudden sharp pain or painful emotion.

He was indeed experiencing the ping of a pang.

"The ping of a pang. Ping pang. Ping pang ping..." he murmured to himself in English, delighting in the elastic, rubbery sound of the words.

Then he frowned as the pang moved and changed its shape, turning from a vague feeling in his torso to a sharper sensation jagging down his left arm…

Before the Star Boy could attempt to assess it, he heard a small but odd sound.

Click-click.

He held still and silent.

Click-click, like a small key turning.

It was immediately followed by a gruff, mechanical splutter.

And then came a deep, grumbling, chest-shaking ROAR!

The Star Boy bolted upright just as several upstairs lights flipped on in Eddie's room and the neighbouring shopkeepers' bedrooms, illuminating the yard and its brick shed and washing line. But, most of all, the bedroom bulbs spotlit the motorcycle that had switched itself on, as if it was ready to hit the road for an adventure, though no key was in the ignition and no rider sat on its cracked leather seat.

The Star Boy scrambled to his feet, staring at the revving vehicle.

Something felt out of kilter, out of control. The motorcycle … the flittering fairy lights … the video message popping up on the TV. Were all these events caused by his energy not being correctly aligned? The Star Boy certainly didn't feel quite like himself all of a sudden.

A wriggle of worry took hold, swirling and looping around his hearts, binding them tight.

Monday:
Keeping
the secret
of Stan

KIKI: Unflusterable

"What is this miracle?" said Kiki's mum, pretending to rub her eyes, as her daughter slouched into the kitchen. "I didn't expect to see you up so early, since school's shut!"

"You TOTALLY look like a zombie, Kiki," muttered Ty. He was sitting at the table, feeding bits of his breakfast cereal to the hamster nuzzled in the crook of his arm.

"Very funny..." Kiki groaned in reply as she collapsed into a chair, dark tight curls spiralling from her topknot in surprising directions. "I was fast asleep – till someone woke me up!"

"Who?" asked Mum.

"Tasmin. She DMd me just now. Look," said Kiki, grumpily holding her phone up.

"Oh," said Mum, coming across to check out the photo of a goofily gorgeous pup, with Tasmin crouched beside it, her eyes bright and excited behind her green-framed glasses, a yellow beanie pulled down over her shiny black bobbed hair. "And what's Tasmin written underneath? *Can't wait till you meet Coco on Wednesday!* Aw, that's nice."

Nice? Tasmin's message had annoyed Kiki for two reasons:

- *it woke her up on a morning when she could have had a lie-in*
- *the fact that Tasmin had DMd at all. She'd never done this before. It felt weird. Too ... matey.*

And now Kiki found herself annoyed by Mum's cheery response. Shouldn't she be more irritated by Dad's girlfriend acting over-the-top friendly like that?

"Can I see the doggy?" asked Ty, bunny-hopping his chair closer to Kiki, and holding the hamster up to view the screen too. "Aw, it's REALLY cute. But how come Dad has a puppy and we don't? Can we get one, Mum, *PLEEEASSEEE*?"

"Nope," said Mum with a firm smile.

"Anyway, it's not *Dad's* dog, is it? It's Tasmin's," Kiki quickly corrected her brother. She had no idea where Tasmin lived, but clearly it was a lot more puppy-friendly that Dad's tiny, gardenless flat above a shop.

Mum gave a little cough.

"What?" said Kiki, glancing up.

"Hmm? Nothing! Just saw the time..." she answered vaguely, scooping up her bag and keys, ready to leave for her shift at the hospital.

"Wednesday's going to be the BEST, though, isn't it?" Ty gabbled enthusiastically. "We get to see Dad AND go to the funfair AND meet Coco! I can't WAIT to see Stan's face when he sees the puppy for real!"

Kiki gritted her teeth. Ty clearly hadn't listened to a word she'd said at the weekend, when she'd explained over and over again how important it was not to mention Stan AT ALL.

"We won't have time to see *anyone else* if we're hanging out with Dad, though, will we?" Kiki said pointedly, glaring at her brother.

"Who's Stan?" Mum muttered distractedly, shrugging her jacket on. "I thought your new friend was called Wes, Kiki?"

"Stan's her friend too, AND mine! OWW!" yelped Ty, as Kiki kicked him under the table.

"And was Stan at this epic movie marathon Eddie let you have over at his place?" said Mum, raising one eyebrow.

"Er, yes," Kiki mumbled, remembering the excuse she and Ty had made for being round at Eddie's so much over the weekend.

"Does he go to your school too?" Kiki noticed Mum's half-curious, half-amused expression when she asked the question. What was that about? Whatever it was, it was irritating. All these questions were irritating too, especially since Kiki didn't have the answers ready.

"HAHA! No, Squeak – that tickles!" Ty giggled, as his hamster disappeared down the front of his school polo shirt.

"Right, Tyreke – put Squeak back in his cage; it's time for school," said Mum. "And Kiki, you're still meeting up with Wes today, are you? What was the plan again?"

"Dunno. Think we'll just go and hang out at the park and watch the fair setting up or something,"

Kiki lied. She couldn't exactly say she'd be spending the day in Eddie's back room teaching an alien how to be a human.

"Lovely. Well, have a good time, darling," said Mum, while shooing Ty towards the door. "Let me know if you hear anything from school, about when it might reopen. And Eddie's right across the road if you need anything. Oh, and don't forget to double-lock the door when you go out."

Kiki's head was too stuffed with Star Boy-related thoughts to listen to all the dos and don'ts. Thoughts about how to train him, how to keep a zip on Ty's runaway mouth, how she and Wes needed to be one hundred per cent *unflusterable* when it came to covering for the Star Boy...

"You all right, Kiki?" Mum asked, as Kiki sank down in her chair, forehead thunking on to the table.

"Uh-huh," Kiki mumbled. "Just really tired."

More like completely and utterly *exhausted* at the idea of being responsible for the safety of a clueless alien.

STAR BOY: The door to Everything Else

The Star Boy sat ramrod straight by the generator, ready and waiting for his training to begin.

He had been ready and waiting since 7.47 a.m., when the October sun rose. It was now 9.30 a.m. and Kiki and Wes were due at noon, but that was fine. He was happy to wait.

"Back in twenty minutes, Stan! Got to grab some spare parts," Eddie called out, barging in through the door that led to the rest of the building. He picked up his keys and his motorcycle helmet from a shelf by the back door, and then exited into the Outside.

As the Star Boy searched his data for the meaning of 'spare parts' the sound of the motorcycle in the yard interrupted his thoughts, bringing with it a memory of last night's unfortunate incident, which had brought Eddie rushing barefoot into the yard. Once Eddie had silenced the growling machine and they were both safely inside, Eddie had suggested that a reboot might resolve the Star Boy's energy glitches. To please his kind host, the Star Boy had agreed that might be an *excellent* idea, while doubting it would have any effect at all. What the Star Boy needed to do was to research his surging issues. And he would ... only not now ... not when he'd just realized that he had the place to himself.

He began lightly sparking with excitement. This was the perfect opportunity to look around, to observe, before Kiki and Wes arrived. He got to his feet and wandered round the room, poking at soft squares called cushions, opening drawers and stroking silver pointy implements called forks. He even tried poking the cushions with the forks, which was quite fun.

Then he realized what might be even more fun: finding out what lay beyond this very room...

What treasures might I come across? the Star Boy wondered, his hearts pulsing wildly as he opened the door to Everything Else.

Straight away, he found himself in a small, squarish space that he quickly identified as a hallway. As well as another door, the most interesting feature of the hall was the staircase. Quickly, he trod up the creaky steps to the area above. The first room he came to on this level was clearly for sleeping and clothing purposes. It contained a bed for recharging upon and also a rail, from which hung several pieces of different-coloured fabric. The lens in the Star Boy's left eye labelled these as pairs of jeans, T-shirts and checked shirts. (They looked startlingly different when hanging limply, and not covering Human bodies.)

As for the second room, it was a bathroom, so called because it contained a large, hollow object known as a bath, which Humans filled with water and sat in till their dirt drifted off.

There were several intriguing items in this room; and, after squeezing a plastic tube that emitted white gloop – paste for teeth-cleaning – and pressing a silver handle on the white lidded chair – a toilet – which made a sudden and exciting waterfall occur in the hole in its base, the Star Boy remembered the other door in the hallway. The one that must lead to the front of the building, where Eddie interacted with Humans who took him their broken things to repair.

The Star Boy hurried back downstairs, pausing his pulses with every step so that, by the time he opened the door into the shop, he was safely invisible to any passing Humans who might peer in through the big glass windows.

Now, standing behind the wooden counter, the Star Boy glanced around. He noted many stored and stacked and obviously faulty items, smaller ones jostling for space on shelves, larger ones resting against the walls. But what caught his eye most was the small sign dangling on the door to the Outside that read OPEN.

Was that an order? An invitation? What would happen if he DID open the door?

The Star Boy could not resist. He walked round the counter and across to the door. Studying the metal bolt, he experimentally slid it open, then turned a handle and found that the door opened with the pleasing jangle of a bell. There, on the opened side of the door, the sign read CLOSED.

How peculiar. The door was *not* closed; it was

clearly now *open*.

The Star Boy went back inside, shutting the door, and again saw the word OPEN on the small sign. So he opened the door once more, and again the sign on *this* side of the open door said CLOSED.

The Star Boy went out on to the pavement and stared at the sign from that angle. He was stumped by the wording. Was it simply a Human joke?

"Oi!"

Kiki! The Star Boy recognized his friend's voice, though not the funny-sounding noise she'd just made.

He turned round and smiled as she ran towards him, although...

• *it occurred to him that he was invisible, so his friend could not see his welcoming smile, and*

• *Kiki was looking the very opposite of happy...*

"Stan!" she hissed, as she came to a breathless stop outside the Electrical Emporium. "You're there, aren't you?"

"Yes! I am here!" he said, standing framed but unseen in the doorway. "What is wrong? You look troubled."

"I was just washing up the breakfast dishes when

I glanced out of the kitchen window and saw all *this*," Kiki hissed again, flicking her hands towards the shop.

"Ah..." said the Star Boy, understanding her meaning. "The door opening and closing, as if by itself. Yes, I can see that it would have appeared strange if any Humans had passed by."

"Not just that!" Kiki muttered, her eyes wide and her head nodding at the plate-glass window. "I mean all the lights, Stan! What did you do?!"

The Star Boy stepped further back and stood by his friend's side, so that he might observe what she did. Which instantly caused him some alarm. The electrical items displayed in the window, along with all the large and small items within the shop were flashing ... their various buttons, dials, control panels and bulbs pulsing with yellow and red, blue and green and white of every intensity. One especially brightly illuminated machine by the counter began to emit loud, cheerful music.

"*SHAKE, RATTLE AND ROLL!*" an American-sounding voice sang out.

"Everything's lighting up like a fairground!" Kiki muttered at speed. "Can you make it stop, Stan?

Like NOW?!"

"But, Kiki, if I *am* causing this disturbance, I cannot think how that might be..."

A grinding noise to the right caught their attention, and both the Star Boy and Kiki turned to see the shutter of Mr Pickle's shop come rattling and clanking down, only to rattle and clank straight back up – and then down again.

"Help! What's going on!" they heard a muffled yell from inside.

"What's happening?" came another shout, this time from the open door of the Busy Bubbles laundrette on the left, where a deafening chugging sound had begun, almost as if a steam train was thundering along the worn lino, ready to burst through the plate-glass window.

"What's that noise?" Kiki asked Mrs Crosby, who'd come running out on to the pavement in alarm.

"ALL the machines have started up!" she called out nervously.

"Stan, you have *got* to try and do something," Kiki hissed, as she hurried into the Electrical Emporium and shut the door. "Can you use your data lens to find out how to fix whatever this is? Are you listening, Stan? *Stan?!*"

The invisible Star Boy was still standing on the pavement.

Any other time, he would have been delighted to realize he could lip-read what his friend *inside* the shop was saying, but right now he was more caught up with witnessing the electrical mayhem and trying to ignore the gnawing ache that had begun in his left hand.

Somehow this was all his fault.

Somehow he was causing distress to Humans, which was the very last thing he ever wanted to do.

Somehow he *had* to find out what was going wrong and make it right, before it got him – and possibly his friends and rescuers – into trouble.

WES: The problem with parallel universes

It was a day of no school, which meant a day less of Wes running the risk of bumping into Harvey and his mates in the corridors. Ace.

And it also meant that Wes could hang out with his new and brilliant friends. He and Kiki would need to spend time training Stan, for sure. But that wouldn't take ALL day. Maybe they could take the Star Boy out for an educational field trip! And, thanks to his conversation with Mrs Crosby yesterday, Wes had an idea about what that could be...

But for now there were less exciting but necessary things to think about.

"Hey, Dad, we're out of milk," said Wes, as he sat at the small table that doubled up as his dad's workspace, waving the empty plastic carton.

"Uh-huh..." muttered Dad, ruffling his unkempt beard.

"Dad!" Wes tried again, reaching over and swivelling the laptop round and away from his father's gaze.

"Hey!" grumbled his dad, reaching out and setting it right again. "I'm just in the middle of doing some research for work!"

Wes stared at his father, whose shirt was so crumpled it looked like it had been slept in.

He knew Dad was lying. He wasn't researching, or trying to find new clients. Dad was playing online Sudoku.

"Do we need other stuff?" Wes tried again. "Do you want to order a delivery from the supermarket? Or should I go to the shops, since school's closed again today?"

"Mmm..." muttered Dad, lost in a parallel universe where he didn't have to think about work that he didn't have, or filling empty cupboards. A parallel universe where all that mattered was slotting numbers tidily into boxes.

Wes knew all about parallel universes too. He read about them all the time, watched TV shows and films about them, played games centred around them.

And then there was his own personal parallel universe ... an alternative version of Wes Life.

The setting was a cottage where a bright-eyed, clean-shaven dad sang along to the radio as he worked on his laptop, designing websites. There was a smiley mum with a white-blond pixie cut, who often left cherry-red kiss marks on the dad's cheek. They were fun, this mum and dad. Proper warm-inside-your-tummy fun. They laughed at each other's jokes and danced round the kitchen.

Wish I could dip into that world right now, thought Wes, starting to pile up the breakfast plates and glasses. Like all good stories, he'd based his parallel universe on something true – the photo albums he'd found tucked at the back of a cupboard, under a pile of old towels, right around the time Mum left. The cottage, the dad, the mum, the fun, the music ... that *had* existed. It *had* happened. Just in a time before Wes. When there was only the two of them.

Things between his mum and dad had somehow started to bend and shift when Wes was tiny. All he remembered of life as a threesome were arguments and silences; Dad locked away in a room working, Mum's unhappy face when she came home from the salon...

"Actually, yes, if you could go to the shops," Dad said vaguely.

Wes stared across the table, trying to remember when Dad had started to properly fade, to turn into a tissue-thin version of himself. It was before Mum left, Wes was pretty sure. Maybe it was one of the reasons she'd gone.

"OK," said Wes, getting up and going over to take some money from the tin on the shelf. "I'm seeing my friends later, so I'll pick the stuff up when I'm out."

"You're going out *again*?" Dad checked, sounding unsure. "Shouldn't you do some studying while school's shut? And who are these friends anyway?"

Wes clenched his teeth. He knew it was hard for Dad to get his head round the idea of Wes having a life away from him, especially after home-schooling his son up until recently.

"We haven't been set any work by our teachers,

Dad," Wes explained patiently. "And my friends are Kiki and Stan. You'd like them."

Even as Wes said that last bit, he knew there was zero chance of Dad ever meeting Kiki and Stan, since he rarely left the flat. And, the way Dad was, Wes wouldn't have dreamed of inviting anyone to visit ever.

"Sometimes I wonder if it was a good idea to let you go to secondary school. I'm sure I could tutor you in some of the subjects, if I put my mind to it," Dad muttered.

The flat suddenly felt airless. It made Wes's chest feel as tight as his asthma sometimes did. He ached for the oxygen of brightness and colour.

And luckily there was a way to make that happen.

With his back still to Dad, Wes tapped a message to Kiki.

Can we meet up earlier than 12?

He'd barely sent the message when he got a reply.

YES! I'm already with Stan. Come now!

Wes grinned. Sometimes he wished he could be a better son and magically make his dad happier. But, if that wasn't possible, at least it was good to be needed by someone.

And for more than just picking up a carton of milk.

STAR BOY: The Learning List

There was a gentle, almost shy tapping at Eddie's back door.

"That will be Wes!" the Star Boy said cheerily, his amber glow intensifying as Kiki bounded off the sofa to let their friend in.

"I am SO glad to see you!" said Kiki, waving Wes inside.

"Hello, Wes! I'm exceptionally *ecstatic* to be in your company again!" said the Star Boy.

"Well, it's good to see you too," Wes replied, as he settled himself down on one of the saggy sofas. "So what have I missed?"

"I have learned to make tea!" announced the Star Boy. "Eddie showed me how. You must stir together a tiny bag of leaves, heated H20 and liquid from a cow! Would you like me to make some for—"

"Hold it!" Kiki interrupted. "Stan, I think Wes needs to know about more important things than that. Like what happened this morning... Which, if it *keeps* happening, is going to make it even harder to hide you."

Of course this was the reason that Kiki was not smiling. She was rightly concerned about the situation. And from the expression on Wes's face he was concerned too. The Star Boy needed to reassure his friends that the problem – whatever it was – was temporary (he hoped).

"Some electrical irregularities have occurred," the Star Boy explained quickly. "I think *perhaps* I might have unwittingly caused them due to energy surges, which are possibly occurring while my system recalibrates in the Earth's atmosphere..."

He watched as Wes looked at Kiki for more information.

"Before you got here, Stan told me that he somehow managed to start Eddie's motorbike in the night – without using the key," said Kiki, crossing her arms. "But, worse than that, this morning Stan was standing outside on the pavement –"

"*Invisibly*," the Star Boy interrupted, hoping that Wes would at least be relieved to know this fact.

"– and the electrical equipment in all three shops in the parade went nuts," Kiki continued.

"Nuts how?" asked Wes.

"The lights of all the kettles and stuff in the front window of the Emporium were flashing; the washing machines in the laundrette all came on; Mr Pickle's shutters were zooming up and down," said Kiki.

"The disturbance only lasted one minute and six seconds," the Star Boy butted in.

"It felt a *lot* longer," said Kiki. "Luckily, Eddie came back and managed to convince Mrs Crosby and Mr Pickle that it was an energy company issue and nothing to worry about."

"Wow," said Wes, taking it all in.

"Wow, wow, WOW," repeated the Star Boy, rolling the lovely word around in his mouth.

"What are you doing?" Kiki asked him.

"'Wow' is a casual expression of astonishment. I can use it in public. It is a word that will make me fit in!" said the Star Boy. "And while we were waiting for you to arrive, Wes, Kiki taught me many other useful things to help me blend in."

"Hold on," said Kiki, "I don't think that's as important as—"

"What useful things, Stan?" asked Wes, his face lighting up with interest. "What's Kiki been teaching you?"

The Star Boy squirmed in his seat a little, as he got ready to list what he had learned.

"One: I must never go into the Outside without both of you. Two: I must try to observe and copy your behaviours when we are in the Outside. Three: I must not use my data lens around people as they might see it scrolling. Four: I must not point at other Humans, as it can annoy them. Five: I must use a quiet voice when observing and discussing people so that I do not seem rude or draw attention to myself. Six: I must always blink my eyes up and down, and *never* from side to side."

"That's great, Stan!" said Wes. "And well done, Kiki – you've pretty much covered everything Stan needs for now. So how about we go out somewhere and let him practise being human?"

"Wait a sec, Wes," said Kiki. "Don't you think it's a bit soon? We haven't even started on a cover story for him!"

The Star Boy saw Wes give a not-worried shrug.

"Why don't we say he's a family friend of Eddie's who's come to stay for a bit? That'll do!" Wes said hurriedly, as he pulled his phone out of his pocket. "Anyway, I thought we could all go to see THIS today!"

The Star Boy couldn't make out what was on the screen of the mobile Wes was holding up towards Kiki. But whatever it was it caused her to frown.

"It'll be fun, Kiki!" said Wes, moving the phone so that the Star Boy could look too.

"This is a *bus shelter*, I think?" said the Star Boy, his all-black eyes squinting and blinking side to side at the screen. "Will this be fun, Kiki? Will I enjoy going to see this structure?"

Kiki rolled her eyes.

"Wes isn't showing us the *bus shelter*," she began to explain. "He's talking about the advert on the *side* of it. For a movie."

"I thought it would be a cool thing for us to do today," said Wes.

"Yeah, but, Wes, I still don't think it's a good idea to—"

"A 'movie'?!" the Star Boy exclaimed over the top of Kiki's words, as he scrolled through data.

"Ah, movies appear on TVs or in cinemas. Would we be going to a cinema?"

"Yes!" replied Wes. "And there's a screening at twelve at the Odeon, so we could easily make that."

"Then I would like to see this earthly marvel very much, please!" the Star Boy announced.

"Great!" said Wes, his eyes like small moons with excitement. "We can get the bus there."

The Star Boy's hearts surged, and he gasped in wonder at the idea of travelling on a bus again. He'd been delighted by their outing on a number 32 last week.

"But won't it be a bit weird?" he heard Kiki ask. "Taking an alien to see, you know, an *alien* movie?"

"Stan'll love it!" Wes said enthusiastically. "It's about this young guy who delivers pizzas to some scientists, and when he's in their building he comes across an alien held captive in a lab, and then there's an accident with chemicals or radiation or whatever, and they swap bodies!"

"This sounds ... most fascinating!" the Star Boy murmured.

"See?" said Wes. "Stan wants to go! It'll be fun to see what you think of it!"

"But what if something happens in the cinema?" Kiki asked, as she looked from the Star Boy to Wes and back again. "What if you have one of these weird power surges, Stan?"

"Nothing will happen. I will be better, Kiki. I will assess my energy constantly, be vigilant for any irregularities and correct them," the Star Boy promised.

"Look, Kiki, you said it yourself yesterday: we *have* to get Stan used to normal life, and that won't happen sitting in here," said Wes. "And, if we go to the movies, we'll be silent and in the dark for most of the time, so it won't be too exhausting for Stan. Or us!"

As Wes worked on Kiki, the Star Boy had already begun to Morph into his Human form, copying the height, skinniness and dark hair colour of Kiki, and the gender and spiked hair of the much shorter Wes.

"Stop!"

The Star Boy paused, wondering why Kiki had called out in what sounded like alarm.

"We need to find you something to wear!"

Ah, yes, of course! Morphing into a Human boy – a naked Human boy – was a 'DON'T' that Kiki should add to the Learning List...

KIKI: Promises and popcorn

Half an hour and a bus ride later, Kiki found herself shuffling into the last three free seats in Row F, Screen 1 at the Odeon multiplex, with an alien disguised as a regular boy (thanks to a loan of some clothes from Eddie), and a regular boy acting like an overexcitable five-year-old.

"This is going to be brilliant!" said Wes, settling down in his seat with his box of nachos and melted cheese.

"Hmm," muttered Kiki, as she glanced around. It felt as if the whole of Riverside Academy was here.

Kiki leaned over the madly grinning Star Boy and hissed at Wes, "You know you CAN take your hood down in here!"

She didn't mean to be mean. She knew Wes well

enough now to understand that his hooded Puffa jacket was like a security blanket for him to hide inside. Only it looked so odd that it tended to attract attention even more. And attracting attention when you were in charge of a trainee human felt risky.

"OK," said Wes, shoving his hood back off his head and freeing his spikes of blond hair.

Feeling better, Kiki shrugged off her own jacket, but just as she was beginning to relax she saw her ex-friends Zainab and Saffron sitting a few rows in front. They were swivelled round in their seats, staring in Kiki's direction, sniggering and whispering together, probably about her choice of new mates.

There was no sign of Lola, though she was bound to be here. Kiki bit her lip nervously; last time she'd seen Lola was on Thursday, at the school's Open Evening. Lola had given Kiki the option to rejoin the Popular Crew – and Kiki had thrown it back in her face by choosing Wes instead. Kiki felt a knot of dread twist in her tummy. How did Lola treat people who'd dared to snub her?

"What are in the paper boxes people are carrying?" she heard the Star Boy ask, as a flurry of latecomers hurried to find their seats.

"Popcorn. It's a kind of snack," Kiki explained, her pulse quickening as she spotted Lola with Harvey Wickes, shuffling along the row to join Zainab and Saffron.

"Snack. *Snack-snack*," repeated the Star Boy, delighting in the word. "Snack-snack-snack-SNACK!"

"Shh! And can you stop bouncing?" Kiki hissed, wishing her friend would sit still, wishing the lights would hurry up and dim.

"Kiki! Those are the unpleasant girls who used to be your friends!" the Star Boy now stated.

"Stan – do you remember what I said earlier about talking too loudly and pointing?" Kiki hissed some more, quickly tugging his arm down.

"Ah, yes. *Don't*," said the Star Boy, recalling rules four and five from the Learning List.

In that moment, Kiki froze, as she and Lola locked eyes. She watched as Lola's smile faded to a dull stare, and with a toss of her ultra-long hair, Lola turned her back to Kiki and took her seat. What did that *mean*? Was Lola planning on blanking her from now on? At least that would be better than being bullied... But it was a bit too early to bet on how

Lola planned on punishing her. She probably hadn't figured out the best way to do it yet.

All of a sudden, the lights began to dim, and Kiki gratefully settled back into her seat. The audience babble dipped away, and the giant screen burst into life.

A millisecond later, several hundred switched-to-silent-mode mobiles *also* burst into life. They vibrated in the hands, laps, pockets and bags of everyone in the Odeon Screen 1, their shimmering screens demanding their owners' attention.

Kiki's stomach twisted itself into an instant knot.

"Stan! What have you done?!" she hissed, scrabbling for her own phone and dreading what message she'd find beaming from it.

WES: How not to relax

"I'm sorry – have I caused this? Is this my fault?" asked the agitated Star Boy.

Around the cinema, a tsunami of groans, *no ways* and *you have GOT to be kidding*s had broken out.

"It's OK, don't panic!" said Wes, though he was panicking himself as he frantically tried to find his own phone. When he finally did a split-second later, he was practically dizzy with relief when he saw that it was a message from school.

"Check it out, Stan," Wes whispered to the Star Boy, while pointing at the message. "All the phones lighting up... It's definitely not your fault!"

"There is an explanation for this activity?" the Star Boy asked anxiously, against a backdrop of sound and colour, as the pre-movie adverts began.

Despite ongoing repairs, Riverside Academy will reopen tomorrow. I look forward to welcoming all students back. Mrs Evans

"I'm sorry I thought you were to blame, Stan," Kiki joined in. "It's just after everything that happened back at Eddie's place..."

"I understand. And I accept your apology, Kiki," said the Star Boy in a voice just loud enough to earn him a shush from the row in front.

"OK, so that's sorted," Wes said, glad he could relax.

Except he couldn't.

For a start – before the lights had gone down – Wes had seen Harvey Wickes twisting round to stare at him from a few rows in front. Harvey had held two fingers up to his eyes, then pointed them menacingly at Wes. The message was simple: 'I'm watching you.'

And now a *second* alert pinged on Wes's phone. No one else had stirred, so it couldn't be a follow-up message from school. Wes guessed pretty much instantly who it was from.

Where are you? When will you be home? the text read.

Wes understood that Dad got angsty when he was out, but it *was* kind of irritating, especially when Dad didn't pay much attention to Wes when he was actually there. And especially since this was his first-ever visit to the cinema with real-life friends.

Be back later this afternoon, Wes texted in reply, then switched his phone off.

As he settled back in his gently bouncy seat, a thought suddenly niggled in his head. Maybe Kiki had a point. Was taking an actual alien to see a sci-fi movie a mistake? What if Stan found it too triggeringly familiar? (He might get upset and dysregulated!) Or what if he thought the whole concept was just too ridiculously wrong? (What if he objected really loudly?)

I'll just have to keep an eye on him, thought Wes, glancing at the Star Boy who was wide-eyed and open-mouthed at an ad for Lynx aftershave.

As he moved his head, Wes felt an ache in his neck and shoulders. He shrugged, trying to loosen his tense muscles, and reminded himself that while this outing *was* kind of stressful it could also be the most awesome experience of his entire life. He'd always loved losing himself in sci-fi stories, and now he was watching one with an actual Star Boy by his side.

Wes let the bright colours and sounds of the cinema wash over him, hardly believing his luck.

STAR BOY: The truth about lies

Hordes of young Humans streamed out of the cinema. At the edge of the crowds, the Star Boy watched as some headed to nearby buildings that advertised items with pleasing words such as 'pizzas' and 'nachos' and 'sushi'.

"Pizzas, nachos, SUSHI! Pizzas, nachos, SUSHI!" he sing-songed to himself as he and his friends passed people joining snaking queues at various bus stops.

"I was thinking we might walk back instead of catching the bus," he heard Wes say. "If we take the walkway over the ring road, you get a great view!"

The Star Boy stared at the large outdoor stairwell and towering structure that they were approaching.

"But only if you have the energy for it, Stan..."

Kiki checked with him.

"I do, thank you," said the Star Boy, now excited by the earthly marvel of metal in front of them.

"So," said Wes, as he began walking up the clanking steps. "What did you think of the film?"

"It was OK," Kiki said with a shrug. "Some good effects. Some lousy acting. Did *you* like it, Stan?"

"Yes, I liked the film *very* much," said the Star Boy, slipping his data lens back in place and concentrating on the dull twanging sound that the steps made as the three friends pounded up them.

But Stan hadn't spoken the truth. He did *not* like the movie or its made-up story. In it, the alien was angry and bad and destroyed things, making a terrible 'ACK-ACK-ACK!' noise as it assaulted random Humans, sending them flying in all directions in slow motion. The Human pizza man was understanding and good, and was relieved in the end that the alien went back to where it belonged in a stolen spacecraft.

The film had made the Star Boy feel more than a little rattled. As if he might never belong or be accepted here on Earth. And that was too difficult to say to his dear friends. Might they grow weary of him too, if he wasn't *always* doing his best...?

"Hey, look," said Wes, stopping now that they had reached the walkway. "See that, Stan?"

Stan quickly gazed at the four lanes of traffic thundering along on the ring road below them. He spotted the green of hills and fields behind the cinema complex and the carpet warehouse and Fairfield Hospital on the other side of the road. But Wes appeared to be pointing out something of specific interest.

"That's called a Ferris wheel. It's part of the funfair," said Wes, pointing to the giant metal shape arcing above the treetops in the distance.

"A Ferris wheel ... a large, circular structure. Used for entertainment," said the Star Boy, simultaneously looking where Wes indicated, while studying the information streaming in front of the storm-grey irises he'd chosen for his Human boy appearance. "Will the funfair now live in the park forever?"

"No! It's just passing through; it's only actually open for one day, then they dismantle the whole thing and move somewhere else," Kiki explained. "It won't be back for another year."

"So to attend the funfair is a very special event?"

asked the Star Boy.

"Absolutely," said Kiki. "Practically everyone in the whole town goes..."

The Star Boy noted a soft, thoughtful kind of sadness in his friend's voice. He quickly scrolled through a list of possible emotions, searching for a match.

"Are you *wistful*, Kiki?" he asked, selecting one.

"What?" Kiki was puzzled by the question.

"*Wistful*, meaning to have or show a feeling of vague or regretful longing," the Star Boy said helpfully.

"No! Yes... I mean, I don't know," said Kiki, shaking her head. "Going to the fair's always been kind of a big deal for my family. But it won't be the same now if Mum's not coming. Not if we're going with Tasmin and her stupid dog instead."

The Star Boy was taken aback at his friend calling a dog stupid, when she had never met it and so would not know if it was stupid or brilliant. And he was suddenly extremely surprised to notice that there was some wetness in Kiki's eyes. He was just about to ask why she was exuding liquid when Wes jumped in with a question.

"Hey, Stan – I wanted to ask you something," he said. "Do you think the alien in the movie was believable?"

The Star Boy thought it was puzzling that Wes was choosing to ignore Kiki's momentary distress. Had he not noticed? But it seemed he had... Out of the corner of his eye, Wes was watching as an embarrassed-looking Kiki turned away and rubbed her eyes with the cuff of her hoodie.

Deciding to copy Wes, the Star Boy pretended he hadn't noticed Kiki's discomfort and considered his answer. Clearly, the alien on the screen was in no way believable – it was just a combination of a Human in a costume and on-screen technical manipulation – but the Star Boy didn't want to disappoint Wes. So he decided to ask a question instead.

"Did the audience understand that they were witnessing a lie?"

"A lie?" repeated Kiki, turning back to the boys.

"The 'movie' was not based on fact," said the Star Boy. "There was no truth to it."

"Well, yes, I suppose *technically* it's a lie, but it's more what we call a 'story'," Wes tried to explain.

"Yeah, and stories are made up, just to be entertaining," Kiki added.

"So stories are *lies*, but they are *entertaining*," Stan repeated slowly. "So Humans find lies entertaining?"

"No – definitely not! Lies are ... well, *bad*," said Kiki, shaking her head, and frowning as she tried to think how to explain things better.

"Your brother Ty tells lies. Does that mean *he* is bad?" the Star Boy asked her, looking concerned.

"No, he's not bad – just annoying," said Kiki. "And his lies are more just stories he makes up."

"This is very confusing..." the Star Boy said thoughtfully.

"And then, of course, you can have *good* lies," added Wes. "They're called white lies."

The Star Boy quickly scrolled. "A 'white lie' is a lie with no malice. Correct?"

"Exactly. It's a lie you tell people to save hurting their feelings," Wes expanded. "It's kind of harmless."

Harmless lies. To save hurting people's feelings. To make them happy, the Star Boy concluded. He considered how upset Kiki had been this morning, when the electrics of the two neighbouring shops had spun out of control. The Star Boy felt terrible about that. Kiki and Wes being happy was the most important thing to him. If he pretended that he understood the surges that were happening around him, if he assured his friends that he could control them ... surely *that* would be a harmless lie?

But the problem was learning the difference between good lies, bad lies and white lies.

Life on Earth.

Passing for a Human.

It was more complicated than the Star Boy had expected.

KIKI: Welcome to the oasis

Kiki and the Star Boy parted ways with Wes on the high street, but almost straight away Kiki's phone pinged with a text from him.

Do you think Stan will be all right when we're at school tomorrow?

Hopefully, Kiki replied, keeping it short.

What else could she say? She had no idea what the Star Boy might get up to, no matter how hard he tried to be good.

"The Oasis Guesthouse," the Star Boy read from the sign that swung on a post outside a building, as he and Kiki started walking up Hill Street.

"That's where Dad stays when he comes back to

Fairfield to visit us," said Kiki, stuffing the phone into her pocket. "Guesthouses and hotels are places people can sleep when they're away from home."

"And what is the meaning of 'oasis', please?" the Star Boy asked.

"An oasis is a watering hole in a desert," said Kiki.

The Star Boy looked confused. "Why is this building named after a hole?"

"A *watering* hole ... like a lake or something. Animals who live in the desert are really grateful to come across one when they're thirsty," said Kiki, struggling to make it clearer. "But it *can* just mean somewhere really nice and welcoming to find when you're tired or your life is a bit difficult."

"Ah!" said the Star Boy, as they continued up the sloping pavement. "Then I think Eddie's home is like an oasis for me!"

"Yeah, I guess it is," said Kiki, spotting Eddie up ahead putting a microwave oven into the boot of a customer's car.

"*Your* home is very welcoming, Kiki," the Star Boy chattered away. "Is Wes's home welcoming too? I should like to see it."

"I've never been," Kiki told him. "I only got to know Wes last week, when *you* turned up!"

"Of course! So my presence facilitated your friendship!" the Star Boy said with obvious delight.

Kiki winced at his overly complicated words. "Yeah, something like that," she said, as they approached the Electrical Emporium, just as Eddie waved his customer off.

"Hello, Eddie!" said the Star Boy. "I am very grateful to you for providing me with an oasis. And, to show my gratitude, I will make you a cup full of tea. Goodbye, Kiki!" He disappeared inside the shop.

"Er, bye!" said Kiki, with a smile and a shrug.

"Good day?" asked Eddie.

"Yeah, things went pretty well," Kiki replied.

"Cool. Any word about when your school is open again?"

"We got a text to say we can start back tomorrow," said Kiki. "But I think the building work will be going on for a while."

"OK..." said Eddie, looking slightly concerned and running his fingers through his scruffy hair.

"That doesn't sound very OK," Kiki said warily.

"What's up?"

"It's nothing really," Eddie said vaguely. "It's just ... er ... I think I've been in shock the last few days, what with ... you know, *everything*. But now I'm getting my head round the whole *alien* thing, I just wanted to ask how it's going to work, like, long-term?"

Kiki pulled a face, not too sure what Eddie was getting at. "How do you mean?"

"Well, Stan's a great guest and really fascinating and everything," said Eddie. "But it is kind of tricky with all the surging disturbing the neighbours. And I've been thinking about the amount of electricity Stan needs to recharge... I checked the meter, and the figures are properly *shooting* up. The next bill is going to be huge if he stays here. And I want to help, I really do, Kiki, but the shop isn't exactly making a fortune..."

"Don't worry," Kiki tried to reassure him. "I'll find out more at school tomorrow. This is only temporary. Stan will be back in the basement soon, I promise!"

Kiki knew her promise was a great big white lie.

And, from the slightly weary smile he was giving her, Eddie knew that too.

Tuesday: The problem with pings and pangs

STAR BOY: KABOOM!

In the dark of the night, the Star Boy had scanned countless pieces of information via his data lens: technical papers, modules and lectures from his planet's most esteemed experts to understand the problems that could arise in a body like his.

Yet he had found exactly *nothing* to explain what was happening to him. Which was most irregular. Where he was from, mysteries were not encouraged. The emblem of the Absolute, and the motto of the planet, translated as *Certainty and practicality at all times.*

But, in the haze of the dawn light, a thought bubbled and brewed and became a plan in the Star Boy's head.

And now, as he stirred, he was eager to put his

plan into action. With his back against the gently humming generator, he turned his head a little to the left and saw Eddie sitting at the wooden table, his breakfasting things muddled with his mending things.

Eddie was currently fixing a large red-and-black cylindrical item, which had a long section that looked quite similar to images the Star Boy had seen of the snout of an elephant.

"What is that?" asked the Star Boy, his data lens already scrolling before Eddie had the chance to answer. "Is it a cleaning device?"

Eddie jerked, nearly dropping the burnt bread he was holding in one hand and the screwdriver in the other. One side of his face was fat, like Ty's hamster. Perhaps Eddie had a cheek pouch, like Squeak, where he stored his breakfast.

"Oh, hi!" mumbled Eddie, as he chewed, gulped and swallowed. "And, yes, it's a vacuum cleaner. They suck up mess from the floor."

His face now back to normal, Eddie wore his usual bright and welcoming expression. The Star Boy was grateful to see it, especially after what had happened the previous evening. At eleven minutes to midnight, to be precise, the large, music-playing machine in the shop had started up, blasting out inappropriately cheerful songs until Eddie came running down the stairs in his underpants and unplugged it from the wall.

"I apologize again for the energy-surge issue. I did not mean to disturb your sleeping section of the day," said the Star Boy.

As he spoke, he felt the now familiar and unsettling ping and pang ripple up and down his left arm, settling as a dull ache in his hand.

"No worries. So how are you getting on researching those surges?" asked Eddie.

"Thank you for your concern. I am making progress."

The Star Boy found himself white-lying, not wanting to worry or disappoint Eddie. The truth of it was he was nowhere near having an answer – but he did have a plan that might lead him closer to one.

"Yeah? That's really great, Stan," said Eddie, as he checked his watch and jumped up from the table. "Oh – didn't realize the time. I've got to take Ty to school today."

"May I come with you?" asked the Star Boy,

visualizing the motorcycle outside. The last time he'd travelled on it was during the high-speed escape from the school playground last Thursday. How he would like to ride on it again, but at a more leisurely pace.

"Hmm, maybe not today, if you're still not quite there with a fix for your, er, surges," said Eddie, grabbing two red helmets from the vegetable rack by the back door.

"Of course, I understand," said the Star Boy, shaking his hand to try and dissipate the aching pain. And then he stopped dead at the sudden sharp noise.

KABOOM!

A torrent of particles exploded from the tube of the unplugged vacuum cleaner. The Star Boy watched in awe as they spread out in the air and rained down upon everything in the room. It reminded him of something. Something he had once witnessed ... a TV show in his Earth Studies class.

The Star Boy and the Others had been learning about the strange Human convention of pairings called 'weddings'. In some parts of the world, it was a tradition to throw many tiny pieces of pastel-coloured paper called 'confetti' over the Humans who had become 'married'.

And what had just blasted out of the vacuum was *exactly* like confetti.

Confetti made of dust, fluff and toast crumbs.

WES: Spotting the shapeshifters

"Can you hear that?" said Dad, perking up like a police dog on duty.

"What?" asked Wes, as he pulled on his backpack, ready to leave for school.

"All that thumping and clattering in the flat next door. Do you think it's squatters? It's been empty since we moved here."

"It could be poltergeists!" Wes tried to make a joke, but Dad didn't even raise a hint of a smile.

"I won't be able to concentrate on work if there's going to be chaos and noise coming from over there," he grumbled.

"It sounds like someone's vacuuming. Perhaps we're getting new neighbours," Wes suggested. "You could always knock and find out."

"I'm hardly going to do that, am I!" said Dad, pulling a what-are-you-talking-about face at Wes.

So no, Dad wasn't likely to do that. Mum was the one who talked to everyone. Wes missed Mum's chattiness. Wes missed Mum. But her life with the toddler twins and the new husband and new salon and living so far away meant their chance for chats was getting rarer. The time between her phone calls was stretching longer and longer, so that Wes wondered if one day the elastic bridging the gap would snap and there'd be nothing there but thin air and silence.

"Well, I'm going now," said Wes, as he walked towards the front door, automatically patting the chest of his Puffa jacket where he kept the tiny treasures that reminded him of Mum. The smooth shell, the star earring, the silver sixpence: they were all tucked safely in his inside pocket, where they gently vibrated to the rhythm of his heartbeat.

"Mmm ... have a good day at school," his dad answered distractedly.

"I'll try," said Wes, feeling his heart sink as he pulled the door closed.

What sort of mood would Dad be in when he

got home? He was down enough as it was, always moaning about how awful Fairfield was compared to their old village. The last thing Wes wanted was for him to start getting wound up by whatever might be happening in the neighbouring flat.

Speaking of neighbours, as Wes came out of the building and down the alleyway, he spotted Lola whatsername emerging from one of the posh houses across the road. She looked different when she wasn't with her crew – like a normal twelve-year-old – yawning and yelling bye to her mum.

Unnoticed by Lola, Wes crossed the street and walked behind her. As soon as she got within sight of the school gates, she pulled on her queen-bee persona like a sparkly jacket, flicking her ultra-long hair over her shoulder, and sashaying along the pavement.

It's funny how people can flip from one version of themselves to another, like shapeshifters, thought Wes, who always felt exactly the same keeping-himself-to-himself loner. Or at least he *did* till he met the Star Boy and Kiki. He'd begun to get braver around the edges whenever he was with them.

Maybe I need to get a bit braver when I'm

WITHOUT them, thought Wes, and tried walking just a tiny bit taller. It felt good.

His hand went up to push back his hood – but that felt too weird, too exposed, like turning up at school in pyjamas.

And then Wes felt a shiver snake down his back, as if he was being watched.

"Stan?" he said hopefully, wondering if the invisible version of the Star Boy – the *ultimate* shapeshifter – was close by. Then it dawned on Wes who was more likely to be spying on him right now. He turned back and waved at Dad, who was leaning far out of the second-floor living-room window, his eyes fixed on Wes.

It was as if Dad lived in permanent fear of something unexpected and awful happening to his son.

And the funny thing was something unexpected had already happened to Wes, but it was the very opposite of awful.

He turned back and hurried off to school, where he could get comfortably lost in the crowds.

KIKI: Coming up with a cover story

As Kiki headed in the direction of breakfast, yet another message from Tasmin zapped through. It was getting to be a habit.

Still, Kiki pressed play on the video, and watched the little black puppy romp around. Yes, it was really cute but Kiki didn't need a daily update. Anyway, it was nearly time to leave for school.

"Hi," Kiki grunted, walking into the kitchen.

"Hi, honey!" said Mum, who was sitting hunched over the table with Ty. "Come and have a look at Ty's homework book, Kiki; your brother's drawn and annotated an alien!"

"A what? An *alien*?" said Kiki, curious at the coincidence of Ty's teacher setting that as homework.

She leaned over to check out what Ty had been

up to – and instantly felt her heart race. On the page was the squiggled outline of a lookalike Star Boy, with arrows and captions in Ty's wibbly handwriting that read: **Skin color oranj, eyes blink side 2 side, super-cool lazer powrs!** dotted round it.

Kiki shook herself – now was not the time to get flustered. She needed to come up with something to play down Ty's all-too-accurate portrayal of their friend.

"Look – you've done it all wrong, Ty. The instructions say to 'Draw and annotate a *friend*'," Kiki said bluntly. "You weren't supposed to make someone up. Especially not some silly extraterrestrial!"

"It was just more fun than drawing Lucas..." Ty muttered, mentioning his real-life best buddy.

"Aw, don't be a meanie, Kiki!" said Mum, wrinkling her nose at her daughter. "It *would* be fun to be friends with an alien, wouldn't it, Ty? And look – you've even named him! Oh ... so he's called Satan?"

"*Stan*," Ty said quickly, keen to correct his spelling mistake.

Kiki's eyes widened at her brother, willing him to shut up.

"Stan ... same as Kiki's new friend?" said Mum, looking highly amused.

The roar and splutter of Eddie's motorbike pulling up outside had never been so welcome.

"I'll take Ty – I'm leaving anyway," said Kiki, shooing her brother out of the kitchen to find his coat.

"I think it's a bit of hero worship," Kiki gabbled at Mum. "Stan's been really good with Ty."

"Mmm," muttered Mum. "Sounds like a very nice boy. I'd love to meet him. Him *and* Wes!"

"Yeah, sure, sometime..." Kiki said vaguely, zooming after her brother as he pulled the front door open and ran outside with a whoop.

Kiki's shoulders sank as she pulled the same door closed behind her.

"How many times have I told you to keep Stan to yourself?" she hissed, as Ty clambered into the sidecar, with Eddie already buckling his helmet in place.

"What's happened?" asked Eddie, looking concerned.

"Ty drew Stan in his alien form for homework and showed it to Mum just now!" Kiki said wearily.

"That's *so* not cool, Ty," said Eddie gently.

"But it's not like I said he was REAL!" Ty protested.

"That's not the point," Kiki tried to explain. "The more you mention Stan, the more you put him at risk. And keeping Stan safe is a *really* important job we've ALL got to do."

"OK. I'm sorry," said Ty, his chin dropping.

"I know you can do it," said Eddie, patting him on the shoulder.

Kiki allowed herself to relax a little. Ty adored Eddie, and would pay more attention to him.

"Hey, Kiki – Stan's surges are still happening," said Eddie, tugging on his helmet. "He told me he was making progress trying to fix them, but then the vacuum cleaner I was fixing just now blew up, and the jukebox started playing Elvis Presley songs in the middle of the night."

"I'm so sorry!" Kiki blurted out, as if the Star Boy's electrical glitching was her fault.

"No worries," said Eddie. "But it would be great if you could try and find out when Stan might be able to go back to your school..."

Kiki winced. This was the second time Eddie had brought the subject up in two days. But if the school basement wasn't ready for weeks, or even months, and Eddie couldn't afford to have Stan stay, what on earth was she meant to do with a homeless alien?

"I'll do my best to find out, promise!" said Kiki, hoping her smile hid the ripples of anxiety she was feeling.

"Wait! STOP!" Ty burst out, his face a picture of concern. "What are you two saying? We ARE going to keep Stan, aren't we?"

"Stan's not a puppy, Ty," Kiki said with a short, sharp frown. "And he can't stay with Eddie forev—"

"Everything all right?" asked Mum, coming out of the front door. "Thought you'd all be gone by now!"

"Just going!" said Eddie, jumping on to the bike and rumbling off, with Ty waving a cheery farewell from the sidecar.

"Me too," said Kiki, before hurrying away herself.

But hurrying was suddenly incredibly hard, almost as if the weight of responsibility for Stan – for keeping him safe – was all on her back, as heavy as a rucksack full of bricks. Kiki forced herself on, eager to get to school and share the worry with Wes.

As she headed down Hill Street, Kiki felt very, very alone.

Except she very, very much wasn't.

STAR BOY: Side by side

The Star Boy waited till Kiki crossed the road and drew level with the Electrical Emporium to fall in step beside her. He had thought to say hello straight away – to tell her about his plan, or a little of it at least – but then noticed the clouded expression on his friend's face. Curious, he tilted his head this way and that, noting Kiki's upside-down mouth, the fur of her eyebrows dipping low on her forehead. What did it signify? What Human emotion was she feeling?

But her face altered slightly, lightened somehow when her phone made a *RING!-RING!* sound. She took it from her pocket and smiled at the screen.

"Hey, Dad," she said.

With the luxury of being unseen, the Star Boy leaned in as they walked, and examined Kiki's father.

He was smiling too, but only with his mouth, not his eyes. Did this mean his smile was not genuine? Or was he perhaps displaying nervousness?

"Hey, Kiki – I just wanted to check in with you before school," he said.

"Yeah? It's funny you should call right now – I'm nearly at the bottom of the hill, and I just passed the Oasis Guesthouse," said Kiki, glancing over at Dad's home from home whenever he visited.

"Ah, well, actually, I won't be staying there this time," said Kiki's father. "I've found an Airbnb that allows dogs. It's up near your school, in fact."

The Star Boy noticed that Kiki seemed a little unsettled by that.

"Oh, OK," she said. "So how come you're calling?"

"Well, the thing is, Kiki, I know Tasmin has been in touch with you the last couple of days," said her father, sounding awkward. "And you – well, you haven't got back to her. She's a bit upset about that... Could you drop her a quick message? Even just some smiley emojis or something?"

The Star Boy turned to Kiki to see her reaction to this request. He was surprised to note that her nostrils were flaring, and she seemed agitated.

"Sorry, I've got to go, Dad," she snapped. "I've just seen my friend Wes."

The screen went blank as Kiki ended the call. Hastily, she shoved the phone back in her pocket.

The Star Boy glanced this way and that.

"Where is Wes?" he asked aloud.

"AHHH!" yelped Kiki, stopping dead and staring around her, trying to locate him. "Stan! What are you doing? You can't creep up on a person like that!"

The Star Boy scrolled 'creep'. It either meant:

• *a scary or odd person (noun); or*
• *to move slowly and carefully without being heard (verb).*

"Do you mean the noun or the verb?" he asked Kiki.

"The what?!" Kiki said, shaking her head in confusion. "Look, what are you doing out here on your own, Stan? It's not safe! You know the rules: no going out without me and Wes!"

The Star Boy nodded, not that his friend could witness that. She thought he had failed at number one on the Learning List. But he had not. Not technically.

"But I am not alone. I am with *you*, Kiki!" he said.

"Well ... you are now, but..." Kiki muttered, flustered. "What are you even doing here? I'm on my way to school!"

"Exactly. Overnight, I have been thinking about the damage done to the building last week, all because of me. I want to see it for myself," he said, telling her the truth, but not the *whole* truth. (*Is that the same as a lie?* he wondered.)

"Not now, though!" said Kiki. "I can take you later."

"But we are halfway there already," the Star Boy reasoned. "I will simply stand outside the railings and quietly observe for a few minutes."

"Stan, I can't let you do this. What if—"

"What if you trust me to do this simple task, Kiki?" the Star Boy reasoned some more. "I know the route back to Eddie's very well. And I promise I will *never* go further afield without you and Wes."

The Star Boy watched Kiki's face soften. She was silent for some moments.

"I suppose I can't blame you for wanting to check out the damage," she said, and began walking again. "But *please* make it quick and don't put yourself in any danger!"

"Yes. I will return straight away," the Star Boy lied outright – ignoring the uncomfortable sensation it caused him.

His white lies – not-the-whole-truths – had a purpose. He very much wanted Kiki to think the best of him, to never wish him to leave. He did not want her to be like the pizza Human of the movie, who was glad when the alien of the story returned to its home planet.

And so he had to find a way to understand the surges and stop them. The Star Boy's plan was this: if he returned to the playground where he had crashed – back where it all began – it might help him focus more clearly on a solution to his unexpected and disruptive disturbance in energy.

It was the only thing he could think of that might help. He didn't dare contemplate what would happen if it didn't. The unknowable awfulness if he was discovered, not just for him but for his dear friends...

"Kiki, why did you lie to your father? About Wes?" the Star Boy asked, suddenly remembering that he wasn't the only one to utter untruths.

His friend rolled her eyes, and carried on walking.

"It's just family stuff. It's complicated," Kiki

mumbled, as they drew level with the high street.

"I'm very grateful that I have grown up without the complication of families," the Star Boy said softly, frowning a little as they passed the movie poster on the side of the bus shelter.

"Look, I can't really talk any more; it's getting busy. People might see me and think I'm talking to myself," said Kiki, as she paused on the kerb.

"I understand," said the Star Boy. "I will walk with you as far as the riverside path. But I will be silent."

With a nod vaguely in his direction, Kiki crossed the high street, then went down the side road that led to the Wouze. At the bridge, dozens of children in uniform were streaming across, all chatting and pointing at what was left of the lower-school playground, visible through the twisted wire-mesh fence.

The Star Boy kept half a step behind Kiki as they joined the throng, dipping this way and that to avoid coming into contact with any of the young Humans. As they spilled out the other side, Kiki paused by the hazard-taped remains of the fence, pretending to look for something in her pocket.

"Stan, are you there?" she said softly, rattling the keys in her pocket.

"Yes," he replied.

"Don't hang around, OK?" Kiki hissed. "Just take a look and go…"

"I will," said the Star Boy.

Even before his friend had walked off, the Star Boy had begun wriggling his way through a gap in the mesh, and now found himself in the disorientating environment of the lower playground. The most startling sight was right in front of him: a huge crater where the large bushes and his hidden-away space pod had once been located. A chaos of shouty yellow-vested people and growling machinery disturbed his formerly peaceful haven.

And then the Star Boy heard a familiar and calming sound … the flapping and cooing of a flutter of pigeons swirling from the ground, welcoming him back.

"It is a good omen," muttered the Star Boy, smiling as the birds spiralled into the air.

Excitement rippled across his chest – just as tiny pings began stuttering and jagging in his finned left hand. Shaking the sensation away, the Star Boy hurried towards the hazard tape, his three hearts full of hope.

WES: How to fit in

Swept up in a swell of blue blazers, Wes pulled the toggles on his hood tighter, as if that would help him hide away just that little bit more.

He scanned the ambling crowds of students all around him as they headed across the playground, and watched them chat easily to each other. Girls and boys laughing, boys landing friendly thumps on each other's arms.

Wes didn't really get how people fitted together so easily. Sometimes it was as if other kids had a secret language that he didn't quite understand. Sometimes he felt like a chicken waddling along with a flock of tall-necked geese.

Is this how Stan feels? it suddenly occurred to him.

The Star Boy was always so cheerful and enthusiastic. But figuring out how to be a human must be hard for him, just like it was for Wes.

Momentarily forgetting the no-phone rule, Wes grabbed his mobile from his pocket, hoping to catch Kiki before they went into school.

"Wesley Noone!" a teacher on duty yelled at him. "Put that phone away! And get that hood down!"

"*Yeah*, Wesley No One!" came a snide voice by his side. "Do as you're told!"

The mobile was flipped out of Wes's hand, quick as a wink, and landed with a clatter on the ground.

Wes dropped down quickly, scrabbling for it before it got trampled underfoot.

So much for hiding in his hood. He'd never be invisible to a bully like Harvey Wickes...

STAR BOY: Where it all began

The work party in the lower playground clattered and busied themselves, unaware of the alien in their midst.

They didn't have a clue that the invisible creature was now descending the small set of concrete steps to the basement boiler room, where the metal door sat wedged open, half blown off its twisted hinges.

And here, where it all began, the Star Boy was relieved to see that, despite a coating of dust and debris, his first and very welcome sanctuary was reassuringly the same, with the large generator intact and clearly still working. He went over to it, lovingly running his hand over the DANGER! HIGH VOLTAGE! sign, instantly feeling at home.

And almost immediately his thoughts turned to

his first faltering attempts at Channelling from this subterranean space. It had given him the ability to remotely wander the corridors and classrooms of the school above, to study the Human students, to learn what they learned. (Algebraic terms! Matisse's abstract leaf cut-outs! Sedimentary rock formations! Life in medieval society! How to make cheese scones!)

In that moment, the Star Boy's hopes of understanding the surges he'd been experiencing were temporarily tucked into a corner of his mind in favour of the lure of remotely wandering the corridors of Riverside Academy once more. Spreading his arms wide across the generator – ignoring the slight ripple of pings in his left arm – the Star Boy thrilled as his senses coursed along the cables and wires of the school, zinging into light fittings, whirling through hand dryers in the loos, zapping into computers, projectors and whiteboards.

He particularly enjoyed zooming into the desk lamp in the head teacher's office, where he witnessed the unpleasant Humans called Harvey and Lola receiving a stern lecture about appropriate behaviour, following the bullying images that had mysteriously interrupted Mrs Evans' presentation at the Open Evening. The Star Boy would enjoy telling Wes and Kiki about that!

And where were his friends? He careered here and there, entering and leaving rooms unnoticed, except for the occasional fizz of static causing surprised "ouches" from the room's inhabitants.

And then, finally ... there was Kiki entering a room on the second floor. Leaving the circuitry of overhead lights in the corridor, the Star Boy zipped into the classroom whiteboard.

From here, he had the perfect view of his friend as she settled herself on a chair. *What will Kiki learn in this session?* he wondered. Whatever fascinating topic it was, he would study alongside her.

The Star Boy only wished that, instead of hiding away unseen, he could interact with Kiki and the other students like a regular boy. What fun that would be!

KIKI: Through alien eyes

Kiki felt a bit sick as she tried to slither as invisibly as possible into her seat.

Sharing a table in form class with people who very probably *hated* her wasn't exactly the highlight of her day. Keen to avoid being blanked again by Lola, she kept her head down and concentrated on rummaging for her pencil case in her backpack. Kiki couldn't wait for lunchtime so she could hurry off and find Wes. She was desperate to discuss Eddie's worries.

"So what did Mrs Evans want you for, Lola?" Kiki heard Zainab ask.

"Nothing important. Tell you later," Lola replied, flicking away the question like a hovering fly.

"ACK-ACK-ACK!"

Glancing over, Kiki saw two boys imitating the alien from the movie while their friends were all bent double, laughing.

"Can we settle down and get started, please?" Ms Naik called out. "We're going to get on with the topic we started last week," she said, tapping the interactive screen and bringing up an image with the word BELONGING on it.

Predictably, Kiki heard a couple of groans and sighs at that announcement, and also a random "ACK-ACK-ACK!" followed by more sniggering.

"Enough!" said Ms Naik, waving her hands to get everyone to settle. "So we've already talked about different types of families and friendship groups, and today we'll be exploring an emotion that's very important in helping us bond with other people. Can someone tell me what that emotion might be?"

Empathy, Kiki guessed, though she didn't want to say it out loud and draw attention to herself.

Ms Naik scanned the room, but no one responded.

"OK, I'll give you a clue. It's to do with standing in someone else's shoes..."

DEFINITELY empathy, thought Kiki, still keeping quiet.

"Anyone?" Ms Naik looked hopefully round the room for a hand in the air. "Come on! Lola – any idea?"

"Dunno, miss," said Lola, flicking her hair and acting extremely bored.

"Well, the answer is *empathy*," the teacher said wearily, clicking on to an image showing the definition of the word.

'The ability to sense what someone else is going through', Kiki silently read.

"We're all different, and sometimes differences can cause difficulties," Ms Naik continued. "But, if we're able to stop for a second and really THINK about what another person is feeling, that can make a huge difference, and really affect their happiness and ours."

Kiki could think of at least three people in this room who had *minus* points in empathy...

"Now I'd like us to come up with a task that will help us develop empathy," Ms Naik said, soldiering on. "Any suggestions?"

The classroom practically creaked under the weight of the silence. Till it was broken by an "ACK-ACK-ACK!" and yet another burst of laughter.

As the teacher tried to marshal everyone back to the topic, Kiki surprised herself by having an idea. And she was even MORE surprised when she found her hand in the air.

"Yes, Kiki?" said the teacher, looking relieved that there was at least one semi-keen student in the class.

"I ... well ... I was thinking about the movie *Through Alien Eyes*," Kiki began, hearing a few whoops at the mention of the film. "It's about empathy."

It suddenly felt as if the whole class was staring at her, wondering where the empathy was in the exciting sci-fi adventure they'd watched.

"Oh yes?" Ms Naik said encouragingly. "I haven't seen it. Can you explain, Kiki?"

"Well, a pizza-delivery guy and an alien swap bodies," Kiki began, feeling a trickle of sweat run down her back, wishing she'd never started. "The pizza guy realizes that the alien acts aggressively cos it's scared and trapped. And the alien sees that not *all* humans are bad. So, you know ... they end up empathizing with each other."

"Fantastic!" said Ms Naik, clapping her hands.

"Unfortunately, we can't swap into each other's bodies, but what we can do is try seeing 'through alien eyes', everyone!"

In that moment, Kiki thought of the Star Boy, who'd be safely back home at Eddie's by now. She'd been feeling so overwhelmed with how to keep him safe that she hadn't thought about how overwhelmed he must be feeling. Moving house was hard. Moving town was hard. Moving galaxies had to be *mind-blowingly* hard. No wonder his energy levels were all over the place. Kiki frowned, silently reminding herself to be more empathetic – and patient – with him from now on.

"I'd like you to split into pairs," she heard Ms Naik continue, "and ask each other questions, so you can understand each other a little better, and perhaps not be so quick to judge."

Kiki watched as Ms Naik started partnering people up before they hesitated or started mucking about and making alien noises.

"...Simon and Bilal, Lola and Kiki, Nancy and Ceyda..."

"Please, miss," Lola began. "I don't want—"

"No discussion, Lola!" Ms Naik said briskly. "Just

get on with it."

With a screeching of dragged and shifted seats, students settled into their pairs. Lola – of course – stayed where she was, letting Kiki bunny-hop her chair closer. Kiki risked glancing across at Lola; she was staring straight ahead, her face like thunder. Kiki sighed inwardly. There was no way Lola was going to be the first to talk. She racked her brains for something to say.

"Erm ... so how's your day going so far?"

The question sounded dumb as soon as the words left her mouth. Kiki readied herself for an epic eye-roll from Lola.

"Well, it's going *fantastically* well, obviously." Lola's words were loaded with sarcasm. "Boring lesson after boring lesson, then getting dragged in to see Mrs Evans about stuff that wasn't even my fault, and now..."

Lola wafted her hand in Kiki's direction.

"Doesn't seem like you're getting on with what I asked you to do, Lola," Ms Naik suddenly interrupted, leaning over the two girls. "Can we get back on topic? Kiki – a question, please?"

With Ms Naik hovering, Kiki's mind's eye scanned

through the events of the last few days for *anything* that might inspire her. And then she remembered the Star Boy trying and failing to show Kiki and the others an image of that important prime-minister-type person – the Supreme? Or the Absolute? – visiting his Education Zone. It was a memory that had clearly left an impression on him.

"So, um … uh … what's your favourite memory from primary school?" Kiki asked Lola. Ms Naik nodded and moved on.

She expected a shrug, and got one. But after a second or two Lola looked up, as if she was mildly intrigued by the question.

"I suppose it was sports day in Year Three," she replied, her mouth softening into a smile. "My nan came to watch and was cheering louder than anyone else."

Kiki stared at her former friend. In the few weeks they'd hung out together, all Lola had ever talked about was fashion, TV shows and TikTok. She'd not once mentioned a nice nan. And Kiki had never seen Lola smile like that – a real smile, not her usual sarky smirk.

"Um…" Kiki began, searching for another

question to ask. "What's your favourite thing to do if you feel fed up? I like to annoy my little brother. That always cheers me up!"

Lola laughed. "I put on my waterproof speaker in the shower and sing along *really* loudly!"

"That sounds ace; I might try that!" said Kiki, not quite believing how engaged Lola was. She felt she had to ask another question quickly before Lola got bored and switched back to her usual mean self.

"So ... er, who's your favourite person?"

"My nan," Lola said without any hesitation. "*Was* my nan. She died last year."

"Oh, I'm sorry," Kiki said, feeling flustered. "Do you miss her?"

She was sure she saw the twinkle of tears glistening in Lola's eyes. It was kind of weird to think that Lola had actual feelings.

"How's it going here, girls?" Ms Naik asked, coming back over before Lola had a chance to answer.

Lola instantly snapped back to her best bored scowl.

"Miss, I don't really get the point of this..." she drawled, folding her arms.

Kiki felt a rush of surprise at the sudden switch-around, even though she'd been waiting for Mean Lola to reappear.

"Maybe if you chose to pay attention, Lola, then—"

A high-pitched whine stopped Ms Naik in her tracks.

"Miss – miss, look! Quick!" one of the boys called out.

Kiki stared across at the interactive screen. Words from the 'Belonging' Powerpoint were zipping backwards and forwards at high speed.

Blended Family, BELONGING, Toxic Friendships, Foster Family, Single-parent Family, Adoptive Family, BELONGING, Bullying, BELONGING, BELONGING, BELONGING, BELONGING, BELONGING...

A clamour of voices bounced round the room.
"Whoa!"
"What's happening?"
"It's aliens!"
"Aliens are attacking the school!"

"ACK-ACK-ACK!"

"Quiet!" Ms Naik shouted, as she hurried over to her laptop. "It's probably something to do with all the building work going on."

As the stream of words flipped and changed, swapped and flashed, Kiki went cold. It was as if they were watching the presentation on fast-forward, the way Stan would absorb information through his data lens.

Stan...

He had kept his promise to go back to Eddie's, hadn't he...?

STAR BOY: A little like a memory?

From the safety of the generator, the Star Boy had been listening intently.

He had been awestruck by Kiki's explanation of the movie's plot. Seeing it through his friend's eyes made him understand the point of the film – as well as the meaning of empathy.

Then he had listened as Kiki and that Lola girl talked about 'memories'. Humans were fond of memories, and could become emotional when recalling them. This was not something that was required or encouraged on his home planet. Imagery was stored on data lenses for practical purposes, with no emotion attached to it.

Except ... except the imagery of the Absolute that he had wanted to show his friends was reasonably vivid to him. Perhaps the closest he had to a Human memory. It was such an auspicious event, an honour indeed that the Absolute had chosen their particular Education Zone to visit.

And, just as that thought ran through his head, the rippling sensation of pings and pangs began to escalate rapidly. They were stronger, *painful* even, tremoring and screeching up and down his left arm, making him gasp, making him jar and judder between invisibility and his alien form, making the whole basement feel as if it was tilting and lurching.

Sharp CRACKS, harsh BOOMS and worrying HISSES exploded and unfurled around him.

And then the Star Boy cut out.

WES: Something strange brewing

There were lots of difficult jobs a person could choose to do, Wes was sure. And being a supply teacher had to be one of the worst.

He sat watching the current supply teacher struggle to get the students to pay attention. Wincing on her behalf, Wes turned and stared out of the window of the first-floor classroom at the grey sky and the buffeting clouds, wondering what the Star Boy was doing right now, wishing he could see him sooner than after school.

A sudden flurry – a twittering and squawk of birds – drove the daydreams away. Plump grey pigeons and flitting little sparrows soared up into the sky in a rush and a bother, as if they knew something strange was brewing.

And then the screams and shouts started. And not just in his classroom – from along the corridor, from classrooms above and below. Wes glanced around in alarm, then froze when he saw the astonishing image on the interactive screen, stuttering on and off like a malfunctioning screensaver.

It was clearly an alien, its skinny body radiating an amber glow against the darkness of wherever it was lurking.

It was hunkered on the floor, its arms spread wide, as if it was about to leap at the screen.

Its huge liquid-black eyes stared straight out at the shocked audience of students and staff, blinking unnervingly from side to side.

Wes stared, dumbstruck, as the screen went blank. A split-second later, the overhead lights hissed, spat and died.

As the agitated chatter of the students reached fever pitch, words whirled through Wes's head.

Stan, what have you done? EVERYONE CAN SEE YOU!

STAR BOY: Running on empty

The basement lights had blown thanks to the colossal surge that had just propelled itself through the Star Boy's body.

Shaking off fragments of shattered glass, he valiantly tried to steady himself, to fully comprehend what had just happened. In that moment of terrible tremoring and pain, the Star Boy had lost control – or felt almost as if something else, something powerful and frightening, was controlling *him*...

And the terrifying reality was that his image – his true self – hadn't just appeared on the screen in Kiki's classroom. It had Channelled its way into every classroom. Hundreds of shocked faces had flashed in front of him in those few dreadful exposing seconds.

Realizing the danger he was now in – visible and clearly alien – the Star Boy quickly paused his pulses as he pushed himself to his feet and staggered out of the wrecked basement.

Now safely invisible once more, he weaved past coughing, gasping workers, all frantically waving away the acrid black smoke wafting from the smouldering, hissing electric cables inside the basement.

His ears ringing with the piercing shriek of fire alarms, the Star Boy sped towards the broken mesh of the fence.

In moments, he was on the riverside path, then the narrow bridge that spanned the Wouze. This very bridge, he reminded himself as he pounded across it, had been the route to safety a few short days ago, when the Others came to destroy all trace of him. And now it would lead him back to the oasis of the Electrical Emporium, where he could hunker down and hide.

IF I can make it there, thought the Star Boy. The agonizing surges he'd felt might well have subsided, but he was exhausted, his energy banks nearly empty. How long could he keep his pulses paused and remain concealed?

If his hearts began to pound, it would be beyond a disaster. His glowing otherworldly self would be visible to every horrified Human in sight.

With no other choice, the Star Boy pushed on with every last spark of energy he possessed. Leaving the bridge behind, he ran up to the high street and launched himself across the busy road through a tiny and risky gap in the traffic.

Finally, he stood at the bottom of Hill Street, looking up towards the row of shops, to the Electrical Emporium, to safety. But that final slight incline, the few minutes more his journey would take ... it felt too much, too exhausting.

Pip-pip-pip...

Panic seized him, as one of his hearts could hold out no longer, setting a patter of pulses free. Swamped with fear, the Star Boy froze, gazing down at his body, which shimmered and stuttered between nothingness and his solid self, glowing amber, then switching again to a bare and unclothed Human boy and back to nothingness.

"Stan!" He heard a shout and a mechanical screech by his side. "Get on – quick!"

The Star Boy turned to see Eddie perched on his motorcycle, some kind of chunky electronic device – a record player? – resting on the seat of his sidecar. Gratefully, he threw himself on the padded seat behind Eddie, wrapping his arms around his waist.

Perhaps it was the relief, but as soon as the motorcycle U-turned and growled back up the hill the Star Boy felt a stillness return, and saw his arms fade fast as invisibility set in once again.

How very lucky I am to have the protection of this kind Human! he thought, as Eddie rode the bike round the back of the row of shops to the refuge of the walled yard.

And then the Star Boy let in the difficult thought he was trying to keep at bay.

What will Kiki and Wes say about what just happened at school? he fretted *How much of a catastrophe have I caused...?*

KIKI: Guess who?

Kiki had never been so glad to see the black blob of Wes's hood. Not that she could go over to him. Not when she was marooned in the crowded playground in her form class's assigned evacuation spot.

But after a muddle of uncertainty – soundtracked by jangling fire alarms and feverish chatter – it was official.

"ATTENTION!" Mrs Evans bellowed through a megaphone. "I'M SENDING YOU ALL HOME FOR THE DAY..."

Practically before the head teacher had finished her announcement, Kiki set off in the direction of the black hood and her friend inside it.

"I can't believe Stan was seen – by *everyone!*" said Kiki, the elongated screech of the ongoing alarm obscuring her words from all but Wes.

The two of them stood looking in the opposite direction from the mass of exiting students, towards the barriers that led to the lower playground.

"That image – it was from the basement, wasn't it? I know it was dark, but I recognized the outline of the generator and the stripes of pipework up the walls," said Wes, blinking fast and talking fast. "But what was Stan even doing there? You told him never to go out without us!"

Kiki winced. "He sort of followed me to school this morning," she confessed.

"What? But how could you let him do that, Kiki?" Wes exclaimed. "You basically helped him break one of your own rules!"

"CAN EVERYONE PLEASE LEAVE *NOW!*" Mrs Evans bellowed through her megaphone, as the sound of approaching emergency sirens droned.

"Look, what's important right now is finding Stan and making sure he's OK," Kiki said urgently.

"KIKI HAMILTON! WESLEY NOONE! LAST WARNING!" Mrs Evans bellowed.

Kiki and Wes reluctantly turned and headed towards the open gates with a few other stragglers.

"We'll just have to hope that Stan managed to get out," said Kiki. "And if he did there's only one place he'd head for, isn't there?"

Without another word, they started running, only slowing five minutes later, halfway up Hill Street, where Kiki realized she'd outpaced her friend.

"You all right?" she checked, glancing over her shoulder to see Wes holding his blue inhaler to his mouth.

"Yeah," he said, speeding up again as his breath eased. "But what's going to happen now the whole school's seen Stan, Kiki? It would've been bad enough at any time, but everyone's still hyped up on that movie. What if people think there's an alien on the loose? What if journalists and TV crews and UFO fans start turning up in Fairfield?"

While Wes talked at a panicked hyperspeed, Kiki stayed silent, sinking under a wave of dread at the idea of Stan being discovered.

And then her spirits lifted a little as they drew level with the shop. Eddie was leaning into the display area of the window, lifting a new kettle out of it, with Mrs Crosby from the laundrette standing behind him. He immediately spotted Kiki and Wes and mouthed the words, "He's here!" at them.

"Oh, thank goodness..." Kiki muttered, pushing open the tinkling door and hurrying inside the Emporium, Wes hot on her heels.

"How much do I owe you?" Mrs Crosby was asking, as she clutched the red kettle in one hand and waved a bank card in the other.

"Pay me later – my card reader isn't working," said Eddie, steering the lady away from the counter and practically nudging her out of the shop.

"That's very kind!" said Mrs Crosby, still hovering in the doorway. "Oh! Hello, Wesley! Shouldn't you be at school?"

"I heard there was a power cut at Riverside... Isn't that right, guys?" said Eddie, jumping in with a plausible excuse, and closing the door as politely as he could in Mrs Crosby's face.

"So Stan's here? Is he OK? And why did you say there was a power cut?" Wes asked, as Eddie turned the OPEN sign to CLOSED.

"Yes, he's here and, yes, he's fine," said Eddie, leading the way round the counter. "And I said it was a power cut because that's *sort* of what it sounded like, when Stan explained what happened."

Eddie was looking remarkably calm for someone who'd been worrying about Stan and his surges just this morning, thought Kiki. Did he know the full story?

"Did Stan tell you that he appeared in front of the whole school?" she asked. "And that he somehow blew all the electrics and shut the place down?"

"Yeah, he did. But it seems *way* too intense to me ... too huge an incident for it to be all his fault. Maybe there was a major problem with the power supply because of all the building work, and when Stan started Channelling, he just *amplified* it."

Kiki really, *really* wanted to believe that, but wasn't totally sure she could.

"But it was a close call," Eddie carried on, dropping his voice for some reason as he paused in the tiny hallway. "I found him at the bottom of the hill, when I was out on a delivery. I saw this sort of ... amber *shimmer* and just slammed on my brakes!"

"He *materialized*?!" Kiki squeaked in alarm, feeling prickles run up her neck at the idea of the Star Boy being visible to yet more people in Fairfield.

"Shh!" whispered Eddie, holding his finger up to his lips. "Honestly, don't worry! No one else saw him."

"And Stan *definitely* wasn't hurt or damaged by what happened, was he?" Wes asked in a normal voice, earning another shush.

"He's just exhausted – he's recharging now," Eddie whispered. "But Stan's pretty stressed out. He thinks he's let you guys down, and that you'll be angry with him!"

"But we're not angry – just worried!" whispered Wes.

Speak for yourself, thought Kiki, whose brain was fogged with a mixture of anger and worry and relief. Yet, now that she knew Stan was safe, the adrenalin of panic was starting to fade from her mind. Which made a much less dramatic question pop into her head.

"Hey, why are we whispering?" she hissed.

"Ah, it's cos your mum's here," Eddie replied.

"She's WHAT?" squawked Kiki, all the adrenalin returning with a wallop. "What's she doing here?!"

"It's fine!" said Eddie, waving at Kiki to calm down. "She heard about your school suddenly closing, and couldn't get in touch with you *or* the school receptionist."

Kiki thought about the phone in her pocket, still switched to school-policy silent.

"Luckily, your mum was only in training meetings today, so she came home," Eddie hurriedly explained. "She popped in here to see if I'd heard anything. I was telling her about the 'power cut' –" Eddie held his fingers in the air to indicate quote marks – "and then Mrs Crosby came in, and your mum said she'd make us a coffee while I was busy."

Kiki glared at Eddie. He really was as clueless as her little brother sometimes.

"So you just let my mum go and hang out in the same room as an *alien*?" she growled.

"Yeah, but Stan's invisible, isn't he, Eddie?" Wes pointed out.

"Exactly! And he's sitting charging by the generator," said Eddie, "so your mum won't have a clue that he's there."

Kiki needed to see for herself that there was no problem. She pushed ahead of Eddie, and burst into the back room.

"Hello, darling!" her mum said brightly, standing by the sink with a tea towel in her hand. "Guess who I've just met?"

Stan – wide-eyed and wearing Eddie's oversized clothes – waved at Kiki and his other startled friends.

STAR BOY: A shy hi

"Hello, Kiki! Hello, Wes!" said the Star Boy, as his friends spilled into the room along with Eddie. "I am having a conversation with Mrs Hamilton!"

"Jackie – just call me Jackie," Kiki's mum replied with a twinkle of a laugh in her voice that made the Star Boy feel happy and at ease. Or as happy and at ease as was possible after appearing in his alien form in front of the entire population of Riverside Academy.

"I am having a conversation with Jackie," the Star Boy repeated, now correctly addressing Kiki's friendly mother. "I have introduced myself. I am Stan Boyd."

As he spoke, the Star Boy observed the expression on Kiki's face in particular, and wondered if he had made an unwise decision to Morph into his Human form.

But how could he resist? Despite the possible catastrophe he'd caused, despite his own depleted energy, when Kiki's mother had walked into the back room, making a pleasant humming noise five minutes ago, the Star Boy had been awestruck. Of course, he recognized her from a photograph Kiki had shown him, and again from having seen her outside Kiki's home first thing this morning.

Leaping up, the Star Boy had sidled over to her, his head tilting this way and that as she stood at the sink, where she tutted and poured water in and out of a dirty cup. He'd sniffed Kiki's mother, identifying the odour of a cleaning material called soap. To be SO very close to a Human adult parent was beyond thrilling! And then the thought came to him that he could – if he hurried – very possibly interact with her. With much haste, the Star Boy had tiptoed from the room, bounded upstairs to Eddie's sleeping and dressing area and thrown on some clothes. He returned with a Human appearance, a broad smile and a shy hi.

"So, Stan ... what have you been chatting to

Jackie about?" Eddie asked, crossing his arms tightly across his chest. His body language appeared to show some nervousness, the Star Boy noted.

"Well, we haven't got beyond introductions, have we?" Kiki's mum said cheerfully. "But it's lovely to meet Kiki's new friends finally. And I'm guessing you're Wes?"

The Star Boy observed Wes nodding. He looked a little frightened. Was he scared of Kiki's mum?

"Uh-huh … this is Wes," he heard Kiki reply.

"Yes! I recognize you from your performance with Kiki at the Open Evening last Thursday, Wes," Kiki's mum said. "Not that you got to perform, thanks to the storm and all the drama!"

I must copy what Kiki and Wes do and say, the Star Boy reminded himself. After all, following the points on the Learning List would keep him safe. And maybe he should copy what Kiki's mum was saying too?

"There was a storm," he repeated. "And lots of drama."

"Yes…" Kiki's mum said with a small, puzzled smile. "It was quite something! So you were there, Stan?"

"No, he wasn't!" Kiki jumped in with a lie before he could answer. "Stan ... doesn't go to our school."

"I don't go to their school," said the Star Boy.

"Ah, I was wondering why you weren't in uniform, Stan," Kiki's mum said with a quick glance at his overly baggy jeans and T-shirt. "Where *do* you go to school?"

The Star Boy had no idea what to say to that. And, for a split second that felt like forever, no one else replied either. It was Wes who finally found his voice.

"He's home-schooled," he blurted out.

"I am home-schooled," repeated the Star Boy.

He saw Kiki shoot him a look that consisted of much frowning.

Perhaps I am copying too closely? he wondered.

"Stan's just moved to Fairfield," Kiki was saying now. "He's ... he's living with a foster family."

The Star Boy was very impressed with the story-making ability of his friends.

"Oh! Did you hear that, Eddie?" said Kiki's mum.

"Ah, yeah! I grew up in foster care too," Eddie said, nodding his head and giving a little there-you-go shrug of his shoulders.

"Isn't that a coincidence, Stan?" Kiki's mum said enthusiastically.

"Yes. It is a remarkable coincidence," the Star Boy replied, playing along.

Then he noted the confusion on Kiki's face. She was clearly unaware of the fact that Eddie had been unable to live with his original family. It was peculiar how Humans could appear to be familiar with one another and yet not know each other very well at all.

"And where have you moved from, Stan?" he heard Kiki's mother ask.

"I am very happy to be in Fairfield. I wish to belong here," the Star Boy replied, sidestepping the question.

"I'm actually quite new too..." he heard Wes say haltingly. "We moved here in the summer."

"Oh really?" said Kiki's mum, turning the spotlight of her smile on Wes.

The Star Boy noted that Wes's pale cheeks pinked up in the glow of that smile.

"It's just me and my dad. Not Mum – she lives up north. I don't really see her so much any more. But we're OK, just me and Dad," Wes said in a rush of explaining.

"Did your dad move here because of work?" asked Kiki's mum.

"No ... not really. Dad doesn't work much," said Wes, blink-blinking and drum-drumming his fingers on his leg. "I was home-schooled before we came to Fairfield and Dad mostly concentrated on that."

"*Another* home-schooler? Like Stan? So many coincidences!" Kiki's mum announced with a wide smile of delight. "Well, Fairfield is a great place to live, isn't it, Kiki? I hope you and your dad are enjoying getting to know it, Wes."

"Dad ... he doesn't go out much. At all, really," Wes said with an embarrassed shrug.

The Star Boy sensed a crackle of awkwardness in the room – but Kiki's mum quickly swept it away with a breezy remark and a megawatt grin.

"I hope my daughter is being a good tour guide, and showing you boys the town!"

"Yes, she is, thank you," said the Star Boy, then felt as if he should add more. "I like the bridges. I enjoyed the one that goes over the many lines of cars."

"He means the walkway over the traffic on the ring road," Kiki quickly explained.

"Kiki!" Mum said with a laugh. "You'll have to take your friends somewhere more exciting than that! What about the funfair tomorrow?"

"Yeah, but Dad's here, isn't he?" Kiki pointed out.

"Well, by the sounds of it, school might be closed again. If that's the case, you and your friends could go in the afternoon," Kiki's mum suggested. "Your dad and Tasmin aren't arriving till teatime."

"I would like this very much!" the Star Boy exclaimed.

"Lovely!" said Kiki's mum. "By the way, Eddie, how do you know Stan?"

Another split-second-but-it-felt-like-forever silence settled over the room.

"Stan's doing some work experience!" Eddie said at last. "He's very interested in anything electrical."

"Oh great!" said Kiki's mum. "You know something, Stan? Work experience changed my life."

"What? You've never mentioned that before, Mum," Kiki jumped in, crinkling her nose.

Once again, the Star Boy mused on the fact that Humans knew surprisingly little about those close to them.

"I spent a week in an office, mostly making cups of tea," Kiki's mum began. "I was so bored! Then the boss collapsed, and I put him in the recovery position – I'd learned that in Guides. When the ambulance came, the paramedic said I'd done exactly the right thing. And that's when I decided to become a nurse!"

The Star Boy listened, enthralled, as Kiki's mum recalled her memory.

An actual memory...

In that moment, a shimmer of an image came to him. It was an odd, unfamiliar and hazy sensation. Was he actually *remembering*? Remembering something about doing the right thing ... about helping people...? Before he could make sense of it, the fleeting fragment vanished.

The Star Boy was still puzzling over it when he felt a sudden ache, like a tight grip on his wrist, with pinpricks shooting into the tips of his Human-shaped fingers. He felt as if he was overheating, as if everything was tilting again. Then the familiar pings and pangs sparked in his chest, and he began to tremble.

"Stan? Stan? Are you OK?" he heard Kiki's mum

ask, his discomfort clearly visible.

"He ... he sometimes gets like this," Eddie said quickly.

"Like what?" asked Kiki's mum.

"Um, Stan can get sort of ... well ... *worked up* about stuff," the Star Boy heard Kiki say now, taking her turn to try and explain away his current tremoring.

"OK..." said Kiki's mum, sounding thoughtful. "Are you feeling anxious, Stan?"

"Perhaps," said Stan, though he didn't know the word, and had removed his data lens before Morphing into Human form.

"Don't you worry. I have some tips for that." Kiki's mum leaned towards him, lifting his clammy hands with her cool fingers. "Can the rest of you give us some space?"

Kiki's mum's chirpy but firm request was met with hesitation. Kiki, Wes and Eddie all stayed exactly where they were, swapping questioning looks.

"Go – all of you!" Kiki's mum ordered. "Eddie, you'll get your work-experience helper back in a few minutes. And Kiki and Wes, you can catch up with your friend another time."

The off-kilter Star Boy watched as his friends and rescuers reluctantly took their leave.

"Right," said Kiki's mum, focusing the full beam of her attention on the Star Boy. "We're going to start with some breathing exercises..."

The Star Boy noticed her blue eyes fix on him. Heard her voice switch from bouncy and friendly to soft and steady.

"Breathe in on the count of four ... one, two, three, four. Now hold for seven..."

As Kiki's mum demonstrated the relaxation technique, the Star Boy followed her instructions, relaxing his pulses to her count.

Slowly, steadily, the pings and pangs, the ripples and the prickles began to ebb.

So is this what having a mother is like? the Star Boy wondered in awe, feeling suddenly very cared for, as if belonging was like someone draping a deliciously cool damp mist round his overheating head and shoulders.

How very, very lucky Kiki was...

KIKI: The spiralling of the 'likes'

Kiki only realized how hard she was chewing her lip when it started to sting.

"What are we going to do?" she asked, as she made her way through the Electrical Emporium and out on to the pavement, followed by a silent Wes.

"Guys, I don't think there's a lot you can do right now," said Eddie, standing in the open doorway of the shop. "Once your mum's done, Kiki, Stan'll need to recharge – he's exhausted. So why don't you two go home? I'll let you know when he's up and about again."

"OK..." Kiki said reluctantly.

"And I guess I'd better get back before Dad hears about school being evacuated, or he'll freak out," said Wes, hefting his backpack on to his shoulders.

"I'll call you later!" Kiki shouted after her friend, as he set off down Hill Street.

"Go on home, Kiki – I've got this," Eddie said.

"But what if Stan says something to Mum that he shouldn't?" Kiki fretted.

"Leave it to me. I'll keep an ear out and get ready to jump in if necessary," Eddie assured her, giving a quick wave as he disappeared back inside.

"Bye," she muttered, her heart sinking at the mess they were all in. No matter how kind Eddie was being right now, she couldn't help wondering if this latest muddle might end up being the point when he ran out of patience with the whole complicated situation...

Ten minutes later, Kiki ran out of patience herself – with Mum.

"Hi, Kiki!" Mum practically sing-songed as she breezed back into the flat.

"Hi," Kiki called out from her perch on the kitchen worktop, where she'd been anxiously watching for Mum to return home. "So ... how's Stan? Did he say anything to you?"

"Ooh, patient confidentiality – can't tell you!" Mum said brightly, tapping her nose.

"I don't mean you have to tell me anything private or – or *medical*," Kiki replied with a frown. "I just mean did you two ... I dunno, *chat* or whatever?"

Mum threw Kiki a clearly amused look.

"We didn't really chat," she assured Kiki. "Stan was just very sweet, and listened to me explaining the tips to help with anxiety."

"Oh, OK, good."

"Anyway, why are you so worried about him saying something to me, Kiki?" Mum asked with that same slight grin she'd worn when she was asking about Stan yesterday.

"I'm not worried!" Kiki protested.

"Look..." said Mum, stopping and staring straight at Kiki, "it's absolutely fine if you have a bit of a crush on Stan."

"*Whaaaaattt?*" Kiki roared.

"So you don't then?"

"NO!" Kiki yelped. "Why would you even think that, Mum?"

"Well, what was I meant to think?" Mum said casually. "I only found out about Stan when Ty mentioned him. You'd never breathed a word about him, Kiki, *or* said he was hanging out with you and Wes. Usually when people do that, it's because they want to keep someone a secret. Perhaps because they have a crush on them!"

Kiki felt her actual secret ache in her chest, just bursting to be shouted out.

Actually, I kept Stan a secret because he's an ALIEN! And now EVERYONE at school's seen him, and I don't know HOW long I can hide him and keep him safe!

How wild would it be to just get that out there? To have Mum help keep this heavy secret with her?

"Look, I *don't* have a crush on Stan! OK?" Kiki said instead, since Mum would never believe the truth.

"OK!" Her mother held up her hands in surrender.

"And, if we're talking about not sharing stuff, how come you've never told me about Eddie growing up in foster care?" Kiki asked, as the thought occurred to her.

"Well, I *have* mentioned it before, but to be honest you've never been very interested in Eddie till lately," said Mum in an infuriatingly calm way.

"Why do you think he enjoys helping out with Ty so much, even though he has the shop to run? He doesn't have a family of his own, so he likes dipping into ours."

Kiki wasn't certain how she felt about that. Their little family felt stretched a bit thin as it was.

"I'm going back over to Eddie's..." said Kiki, jumping down from the worktop.

"No, you're not. I told Stan to go home and get some rest," Mum said in her firmest I-know-what's-best voice. "Eddie's going to make sure he does that."

Mum had no idea that going home meant Stan staying *exactly* where she'd left him. Kiki could picture him now, leaning back against the generator, disappearing into one of his prolonged recharging blank-outs.

"Well, I'm going to my room," Kiki muttered, heading off along the corridor. She already felt exhausted by today, and it was only halfway through. She needed peace and quiet and time to think.

"Actually, since I'm home early and you've no school, Kiki, I thought maybe we could—"

A message alert grabbed Kiki's attention and she

tuned out Mum's voice. It was from Wes.

Passed some Yr 10s on the way home – they were talking about something to do with 'the alien' and Instagram. I'm only on Insta for Dr Who fan stuff and don't follow anyone from school. Can you check?

With her heart sinking, Kiki immediately jumped on to her feed. After a tense few seconds of scrolling, there it was. The stuttering image of the Star Boy on the school's interactive screens had only lasted moments, but in that tiny sliver of time a girl in her year had managed to snap the screen. And there was Stan, in his alien form, hunched down with arms outstretched, glowing and definitely not-of-this-world.

Kiki noted the likes; the count was climbing, spiralling before her very eyes. It was already well over a thousand, which meant strangers outside school were seeing this.

"No, no, no, *no!*" Kiki muttered, taking a screenshot of the post and the ever-increasing likes and sending it to Wes.

When her phone immediately jangled, she supposed it was him – then realized it was the *RING!-RING!* alert of an incoming FaceTime call from her dad.

"Hey, Dad, I can't really talk – I'm right in the middle of something," Kiki said quickly, as his face filled the screen.

"OK, but I just needed to check in with you," said Dad. "I got a text from your school saying it had shut again 'due to unforeseen circumstances'. What's going on?"

"It's fine – it was just a power cut," Kiki said distractedly, suddenly spotting something unexpected in her father's kitchen. "What's going on with *you*? Shouldn't you be at work right now? And why do you have all those cardboard boxes?"

"Oh, hi, Kiki!" a voice butted in, and Tasmin leaned into the small screen, scrunching bubble wrap around a tall blue glass tumbler – Ty's favourite when they went to stay. "I'm just helping your dad pack!"

"Why?" asked Kiki, her jaw tightening, as the sound of sharp puppy barks made it hard to hear what Dad said next.

"I *was* going to tell you and Ty tomorrow in person," he began, running his hand over his shaven brown head. "It's just that me and Tasmin ... we're moving in together. Well, *I'm* moving to Tasmin's flat next week."

Kiki stared at Dad's apologetic face. She barely noticed how Tasmin was looking. And, as her blood quickly flamed to boiling point, Kiki felt furious with someone who wasn't even in the room.

"Mum knew, didn't she?" Kiki blurted out, remembering breakfast time yesterday, and Mum coughing in a telling, *awkward* sort of way when Kiki reminded Ty that the new puppy had nothing to do with Dad. Only it did, didn't it? He and Tasmin and Coco ... they'd be this cosy little family, in some random flat that Kiki and Ty had never seen before. She and her little brother would be more like visitors when they went up to see Dad from now on. Just visitors in his new life.

"Well, yes, I did tell your mum about it first," said Dad. "I just thought—"

And Mum didn't think to let me know? To give me a heads-up? Kiki raged to herself.

"Got to go, Dad," said Kiki, pressing the end-call

button before her father got the chance to bluster a goodbye.

Honestly, if I could sack them BOTH as parents, I would! Kiki grumbled to herself as she tumbled backwards on to the bed.

Mum, Dad, Tasmin ... never mind a slightly malfunctioning alien who'd just outed himself to the world and was about to trend on social media.

Everything was going hideously wrong in Kiki's life.

WES: Sort of wonderful

Wes shook his mobile – he was in a dead spot for reception. Whatever image Kiki had sent through wouldn't download, and when he tried to call her the line was busy.

Can't see what you sent ... try again? he messaged, as he approached the turning to his road.

His brain felt in a dead spot too with everything that had happened this morning. The chaos at school, the Star Boy appearing on-screen and then again in Eddie's back room, right in front of Kiki's mum...

And yet he couldn't blame Stan for letting his guard down in front of Mrs Hamilton.

She seems sort of ... wonderful, thought Wes, as

he stopped at the corner of his road and checked his phone again.

Jackie, he reminded himself. So what was it that made him like her so much, so instantly? Wes compiled a short mental note of her good points:

- *she was funny*
- *she was kind*
- *she made you feel interesting and worth listening to.*

Kiki had no idea how lucky she was.

Without thinking about it, Wes patted his jacket, right where his tiny treasures were stored in the inside pocket. A rush of memories shuffled untidily into his head. Memories of a time when his *own* mum had been funny and kind and made him feel worth listening to. A time before she met her new husband, who wasn't wild about having a stepson. And definitely before Wes was squeezed out by the cuteness of his tiny half-sisters.

But then Wes thought of today. No matter how complicated things were, and no matter how tricky and difficult things might get after this, he'd never, ever regret getting to know all the brilliant people who'd come into his life lately.

With that in mind, for the second time that day, Wes walked that little bit taller, stretching his neck as far as his tight hood would allow, which wasn't much. So he did something drastic and tipped the hood back off his head, setting free his tufts of hair.

Wes glanced again at his phone – the reception had improved, but there was nothing yet from Kiki. Was there maybe someone else he could contact while he was waiting?

Wes couldn't think how long it had been since his mum had last called for a chat, but what was the point of counting, of looking back? This was *now*.

Biting his lip, he tapped and scrolled and found himself staring at the two entries for her on his contacts page. Without giving himself time to bottle out, he pressed one.

MUM (WORK)

As he lifted the phone to his ear, Wes heard the ring, knowing it would be buzzing in his mum's busy salon. Already this felt amazing. If Wes was brave enough to do this today, who knew what he'd be capable of tomorrow?

"Hello ... Mum?" he said, as the phone was picked up.

Wednesday: The mystery of memories

STAR BOY: Rattling and roaring

To 'sleep like a log' was English for a deep and undisturbed rest. In Latvian, it translated as 'sleep like a bear'; in Indonesian, 'sleep like a water buffalo'; and, in Romanian, 'sleep like the earth'...

The Star Boy had researched these alternative terms and many more, yet wasn't convinced that any adequately described the sensation of falling into the blank, unconscious recharging session that had lasted from the time Kiki's mother left until the early hours of the next morning.

But during that long, deep rest he *had* experienced something odd: a blur of tantalizing sights, sounds, sensations. Fragments that blinked into his mind like some stuttering live video:

- *cheering crowds*
- *a presence by his side*
- *a steady, reassuring voice in his ear*
- *a short, sharp pain.*

From this peculiar state, the Star Boy had jerked into consciousness, realizing that the fragments all seemed to be linked to the occasion of the Absolute's visit to the Education Zone. And that immediately made him remember a visit he himself made to a very different Education Zone: Riverside Academy. The awfulness of appearing in front of the whole of Kiki and Wes's school yesterday hit him in the chest like an electric shock.

What dreadful consequences might there be today? the Star Boy worried.

His three hearts racing, he'd used the quietening techniques taught to him by Kiki's mother. Over and over again, he slowed and released his pulses, counting his way to calmness as the still of the early morning shifted into the bustling busyness of the new day, with distant traffic droning and birds chirping their songs.

With his head finally clear, the Star Boy became aware of some friendly voices outside in the yard.

Scrambling to his feet, he reached for his tossed-in-the-corner Human clothes – quickly Morphing into Stan as he pulled them on – and was soon hurrying into the Outside. He was thrilled to find a friendly welcome awaiting him in the brick-walled yard.

"HIYA!" said Ty, waving from the sidecar of the motorcycle.

"Hello!" said the Star Boy.

"All right, Stan?" Eddie called out.

"Yes, thank you. There are some problems to address today, but I am well rested."

"Glad to hear that," said Eddie. "You know, I always think better when I step *away* from problems I'm trying to solve."

The Star Boy smiled questioningly at the young man, uncertain what he meant.

But Eddie had turned away and walked over to the nearby brick shed. The Star Boy watched as Eddie opened its wooden door and grabbed something from inside. He held out a shiny domed item.

"Here, put it on," Eddie urged cheerfully.

The Star Boy stared at the white helmet he had been given.

"YAY! Are you coming to drop me off at school, Stan?!" Ty yelped, bouncing in his seat and making the sidecar rock.

"He is," said Eddie

"Is this true?" asked the startled Star Boy. "Are you sure this will be acceptable to Kiki and Wes? According to the Learning List, I am not allowed to go into the Outside without them..."

"I'm pretty sure they'd consider me an appropriate guardian." Eddie grinned as he plonked the helmet on to the Star Boy's head and adjusted the strap under his chin. "And we're not going to interact with anyone; we're just going to take Ty to school..."

The Star Boy nodded, reassured and beyond excited. His previous two rides on Eddie's vehicle were rescue missions. He could hardly wait to experience this wonder as pure pleasure!

"Does it fit all right?" asked Eddie, tugging at the strap.

The Star Boy used his new talent of lip-reading to answer the question, looking out from behind the clear plastic visor of the helmet.

"Yes," he said certainly, though he had no experience of protective motorcycle hats. Was *so* tight that his Human-shaped ears were squashed completely flat the correct fit?

"Well, let's go!" The Star Boy made out Eddie's words, as the young man clambered on to the old motorcycle, and nodded for the Star Boy to jump up behind him.

With his arms tight around Eddie's waist, the Star Boy thrilled as they rattled off down the hill and along the high street. The experience of travelling on the motorcycle was considerably different to when he travelled on it in a state of high alert and panic. On this trip, he found himself tuning into the sensation of the engine, the thrumming of it soothing him as much as Kiki's mother's calming tips.

He felt distinctly energized as they drew parallel to the river. In the distance, he could make out the leafy domes of the trees in the park, with the giant metal circles and spikes and structures of the funfair rising up behind them like a magical city. The Star Boy suddenly wished more than anything that he might explore this world within a world, to see its ghostly train and sit on the wheel that spun in the sky…

And perhaps I might! he thought, his worries

shrinking as positivity roared through his body in time with the growled rhythm of the motorcycle's engine.

"Hello! It is a beautiful day!" he called out to the small children and adults trotting towards the primary school, just as a light drizzle began.

The Star Boy waved madly, as if he had not a care in the world. And perhaps he didn't; perhaps there was nothing to worry about, he thought to himself. Perhaps everyone had forgotten all about his accidental appearance already!

WES: Pointless

OMG, I swear I saw the alien staring at me out of the food-tech classroom window when we were evacuated from school!

My sister has a friend who knows someone who saw it slithering down the alley next to the chip shop!

It ran past my house, all orange and glowing! My sister said it was just next door's golden retriever, but it WAS ON TWO LEGS!

The Star Boy had gone viral. Not that he knew, and not that he'd understand what that meant, thought Wes, if he and Kiki *did* tell him.

Yesterday afternoon, they had sat in their separate bedrooms, having long, helpless and hopeless FaceTime conversations about the sighting of Stan at school. And all through the evening Wes had been glued to his phone, waiting for Kiki to update him about the fevered alien gossip on students' social media and the latest, frighteningly huge total of likes for Stan's screenshot on Instagram.

Are you awake yet? Wes messaged Kiki now, noticing from the kitchen clock that it was nearly noon already. He wouldn't blame her if she was hiding under her duvet and not wanting to come out till the whole messy situation had gone away.

As he waited for a response, Wes's thoughts turned to someone else he was aching to hear from.

Yesterday's phone conversation with his mum had been short: "*Oh, Wes, darling! What a lovely surprise!*" Mum had said, sounding pleased but distracted. "*Listen, I'm with a client just now – can I call you back this evening?*"

Later, there'd been a text, not a call. **Sorry, hon – twins are TOTALLY full on tonight ... catch you tomorrow?**

And now it was tomorrow, and so far there'd been no text, no call. There was nothing for Wes to do but eat another spoonful from the bowl in front of him. Lunch was cereal. He had thought about defrosting a lasagne he'd made, but it seemed a waste if Dad might not eat some too. (He still hadn't come out of his bedroom.)

Was *everyone* asleep today?

"Morning," said Dad, finally shuffling into the kitchen, wearing his tatty dressing gown and baggy tracksuit bottoms. He stopped dead, tilting his head to one side. "What's that?"

Wes listened too. He'd been vaguely aware of some more bumping and clattering going on in the empty flat next door, similar to yesterday. Now he realized the noise – however low-key – was bound to wind Dad up.

"Hey, Dad ... I've been set some homework. Want to help me with it?" he said in an attempt to distract his father.

"Homework?" said Dad, sitting down opposite Wes at the small table. "What is it?"

"It's a project we have to do called *Through Alien Eyes*," Wes explained.

"*Through Alien Eyes...?*" Dad repeated, frowning. "Like that sci-fi movie that's on at the cinema?"

"Yeah, it's inspired by that. In our form classes, we're learning about empathy and seeing other people's points of view. My friend Kiki mentioned the film as an example in *her* class, and now all the Year Seven form classes are using it for homework," said Wes, as he searched on his phone for the instructions his teacher had just sent through. "So we're meant to pair up with a family member or a friend and ask each other a bunch of questions."

"What sort of questions?" Dad asked warily.

"Um, number one ... name something that makes you happy; number two, name something you wish for; number three, do you have any phobias? Number four—"

"Hold up!" said Dad, his hand in the air. "This isn't what I'd call *proper* homework. In fact, to answer number three, *my* phobia is stupid projects like this, when you could be learning something useful!"

He got up from the table and shuffled off towards

the pile of last night's dishes in the sink. That was the end of it – conversation closed.

Wes slumped in his seat. Asking Dad to help him had started off as a distraction, but, as soon as Wes began reading out the instructions, he'd found himself hoping that doing the homework together might start them talking. *Honestly* talking, and maybe understanding each other better. That hadn't happened for a long time.

As for that first question – what *would* make Wes happy? Simple: Dad being happier.

"Some of the stuff they teach you kids nowadays … totally pointless," Dad grumbled, clattering dishes around.

"Yeah, maybe it is a bit pointless," Wes mumbled, giving up on the list, on his dad, on his mum, and pushing the half-finished bowl away. "I'm going out…"

"Wesley! Where are you going? Come back here!" Dad called, as Wes grabbed his Puffa jacket and headed out of the front door, nearly tripping over a pile of bags outside the flat across the landing.

"Sorry!" he heard a woman's voice call after him,

but his hood was firmly up and he thundered down the stairs without looking back.

As he pulled open the main front door and headed out into the bin-lined side alley, Wes's phone rang.

He hoped it was Kiki. He hoped it was Mum.

Instead, when he looked at the screen, it was a number he didn't recognize.

"Hello?" he said warily.

"WES! IT IS STAN BOYD MAKING CONTACT WITH YOU!" the Star Boy shouted.

"Huh? How did you get a phone?"

"EDDIE FOUND IT IN A DRAWER IN HIS SHOP AND HAS GIFTED IT TO ME," said the Star Boy. "HE SAYS IT IS CALLED A BRICK PHONE!"

"Wow, that's nice of Eddie," Wes said with a smile. "How are you feeling today, Stan? After yesterday, I mean?"

"I AM VERY RESTED AND FEEL VERY STABLE. I AM EXTREMELY REGRETFUL ABOUT YESTERDAY'S INCIDENT, BUT, AS YOU KNOW, EDDIE HAS EXPLAINED IT MIGHT NOT HAVE BEEN MY FAULT. OR NOT COMPLETELY. THEREFORE, I AM CERTAIN THAT IT WOULD BE BOTH SAFE AND

EDUCATIONAL FOR ME TO GO TO THE FUNFAIR TODAY."

Wes paused for a second, thinking of the fevered social-media posts about the alien-on-the-loose in Fairfield. He didn't dare imagine the hysteria if people found out there was an alien-on-the-prowl at the funfair...

Then again, if the Star Boy wandered among them in his human form, no one would pay the slightest attention to some teenager in a checked shirt, hoodie and jeans.

But no – it was too risky, and Wes needed to explain that.

"The thing is, Stan—"

"I WISH TO GO ON THE FERRIS WHEEL AND THE GHOSTLY TRAIN. AND I HAVE BEEN RESEARCHING OTHER RIDES THAT ARE COMMONLY AVAILABLE AT FUNFAIRS, AND I WOULD LIKE TO GO ON A CAROUSEL AND DODGEMS AND –"

"Stan!" Wes tried to interject.

"– AND SWINGBOATS AND CHAIR-O-PLANES AND..."

As Wes listened to the long wish list of rides, he

couldn't help feeling sunnier inside, infected by the Star Boy's enthusiasm. The truth was Wes wanted to experience the bright lights and attractions of the funfair every bit as much as his alien friend did. So while Wes knew that he absolutely, definitely needed to tell the Star Boy 'no', he found himself saying the exact opposite.

"OK, OK!" he said loudly, over the top of the Star Boy's endless suggestions. "Let's do it!"

"EXCELLENT!" said the Star Boy. "I AM READY NOW!"

"Hold on!" Wes laughed. "We have to make a plan first..."

As Wes started walking and talking, he tried *not* to picture the storm clouds on Kiki's face when she found out...

KIKI: Wide-awake bad dreams

"Kiki!" said Mum, shaking her awake. "C'mon, Sleeping Beauty! It's nearly midday!"

"*Nooo...*" Kiki groaned, grumpy at being woken up after a rubbish night's sleep, her mind crowded with jabbering thoughts. And like all middle-of-the-night thoughts they ran wild, magnifying her problems to epic proportions.

Kiki had pictured secret government scientists descending on Fairfield, armed with alien-tracking devices; herself and Wes being interrogated about Stan's whereabouts, with piercing spotlights trained on their eyes; Stan being dragged out of Eddie's, crying out for her as he was bundled into the back of a van with blacked-out windows...

And, when she wasn't thinking dark and dreadful

thoughts about Stan, Kiki was fretting about Dad. In her fevered state, she imagined Dad giving her an ultimatum: be friendly and loving towards Tasmin, or Kiki would never see him again.

Finally, some sleep must have rolled in, with dreams swirling and mixing everything together in a disorientated muddle. Kiki was at the funfair, Wes by her side in a dodgem car. Tinny music blared; colourful dodgems darted round them, and in one of them were Dad and Tasmin. But, no matter how hard she steered and veered, Kiki could never catch up with them. She looked to Wes for advice, but he'd pulled the toggles on his hood so tight that his face had disappeared completely. Then above the tinny music she could hear the panicked voice of Stan yelling her name over and over and over again, till—

"Kiki! KIKI! Come on, lazybones!" Mum persisted, sitting down on the edge of the bed.

"Go away ... let me sleep. Please," muttered Kiki.

"I'm not going anywhere," said Mum, laying a hand on Kiki's back. "Dad texted me this morning, and mentioned that you might've been a bit upset yesterday about his news."

Kiki felt the uncomfortable twist of a knot in her stomach. It might have been a year already, but it still felt like only five minutes since Dad moved away.

"It's OK to feel a bit shaken up with everything changing, you know," Mum carried on, her voice soft and comforting.

Kiki suddenly felt awake enough to be angry.

"But the problem is you *knew*!" she said to Mum, pushing herself upright. "Why didn't you tell me about Dad and Tasmin moving in together?"

"But, Kiki, it wasn't my news to tell," Mum reasoned. "It was up to Dad to share it with you. He just wanted to give me a heads-up in case you and Ty wanted to talk about it with me once he'd had a chat with you both."

"But what's there to talk about? Dad's made his decision, so I just have to suck it up, don't I?" said Kiki, flopping back on her pillows and folding her arms tightly across her chest. "Anyway, why are you at home? Shouldn't you be at work?"

"I swapped shifts," Mum said with an easy-going shrug. "And just as well or you might have slept all day. And you'd have missed your visitors..."

Kiki frowned as much as Mum was smiling. "What? Who?"

"Wes and Stan are in the kitchen. They're all set to go to the funfair, so you might want to shower and get ready."

"What? Why didn't Wes call me?" Kiki babbled, throwing her duvet aside, pulling on her fluffy grey dressing gown and wondering what her (human) friend was playing at. Wes HAD to know this was a totally insane idea!

"Maybe because your phone's dead?" said Mum, pointing to the mobile on the bedside table – its lead was connected to the charger, but the switch in the wall was off. She leaned over and flicked it on.

Kiki felt her chest tighten with the stress of the situation. How could Wes be so irresponsible? Had he forgotten the implications of Stan's image going viral? And that wasn't all – what if Eddie had finally decided enough was enough and he didn't feel able to hide an alien any more?

As Kiki hurriedly tied the squishy belt of her dressing gown and padded along the corridor to the kitchen, it occurred to her that she hadn't even told

Wes about that second point. The disaster of Stan appearing in front of the school – and potentially millions of people around the world – had majorly overshadowed it.

"Hey, Kiki!" said Wes.

"Hey, Kiki!" the Star Boy repeated.

Kiki narrowed her eyes at Wes and Stan, who were sitting at the table and looking exactly like two ordinary twelve-year-old boys, with not a care in the world. Wes was even halfway through eating a biscuit.

"What are you doing here?" she asked in as neutral a voice as she could manage, since Mum was right behind her.

"We're here to collect you, to go to the funfair!" said Wes, with a wide grin.

"We're very excited. And look – I have a phone!" said the Star Boy, holding up his 'new' mobile. "I believe funfairs are quite crowded, so it's sensible to have one in case we get separated!"

Kiki didn't know where to start. Maybe with an excuse.

"But I can't go with you – I've already arranged to go with my dad, like we always do," she said curtly, hoping it was enough.

"Don't be silly, darling! You can hang out all afternoon with your friends and meet up with Dad later," said Mum.

Kiki tried to come up with a better argument, but couldn't think straight.

"Now, boys, you are most welcome to wait here while Kiki goes and gets herself ready," Mum said brightly. "Have as many biscuits as you want."

"I wish to have no biscuits, thank you," Stan said very politely.

"I will!" said Wes, jumping in to cover up Stan's oddness.

Kiki's mum smiled, then turned to Kiki. "Hasn't this worked out well?" she said. "Oh, and here –"

Mum reached for her purse on the counter.

"– treat yourselves to a few rides on me!"

"Er, thanks, Mum..." said Kiki, feeling well and truly backed into a corner.

Tucking the offered notes into her dressing-gown pocket, she turned and hurried back along the corridor, hoping today wasn't going to be as much of a nightmare as she dreaded.

WES: The trouble with truth

The funfair sat right in the heart of the normally peaceful park.

Wes marvelled at its garish colour and noise as he, Stan and Kiki wandered through the milling crowds, mostly made up of Riverside Academy students.

All around them, music blasted and overlapped, different tunes twanging out of speakers on each of the rides. Stallholders yelled at passers-by to try their luck on the coconut shy, hook-a-duck, ball-in-a-bucket and a dazzling array of other silly fun games. Bells rang and horns tooted on the little kids' amusements; cackles and whoo-hoos burst out of the ghost-train entrance.

"This is the worst idea ever," Kiki moaned by

Wes's side.

"It's fine! Like I keep telling you, Stan's feeling really stable, and we'll only stay a little while," said Wes, gawping around and drinking everything in.

Though, if he was being *totally* honest with Kiki, he was finding it a slightly bewildering mix of brilliant and overwhelming.

"Which of these amusements may I experience first, please?" he heard the Star Boy ask. Wes noticed that Stan seemed just as overwhelmed, blinking almost as rapidly as he was.

"Might as well be this one," Kiki said resignedly, leading the way towards the hall of mirrors. "At least we'll be hidden away from everyone."

But two minutes later, as the three of them stood in front of the wonky mirrors, looking at the maddest versions of themselves, Wes heard Kiki giggle in spite of herself.

"Hey, you're Elastigirl from *The Incredibles*!" he laughed, pointing at her reflection. Kiki stood taller than ever, like a rubber toy that had been stretched longways.

"Well, at least that's pretty cool. *You* look like a bowling ball!" Kiki teased back. Wes's mirror had magically turned him and his hooded jacket into a big black sphere with a dot of a pale face.

"I am like ... like a wave!" the Star Boy exclaimed, moving from side to side, watching himself zigzag. And then he stopped, looking uncertain.

"Feeling dizzy?" asked Wes, reaching out to steady him.

"Mmm..." muttered the Star Boy.

"C'mon – let's get out of here," Wes suggested. "There's loads more to see."

Stepping out of the hall of mirrors, the sights and sounds and smells of the funfair once again hit them full in the face.

"What is this, please?" asked the Star Boy, stopping at one of the stalls. Like all the fairground workers, the tall bearded man who was serving was wearing a pair of lookalike alien antennae deely boppers on his head.

"It's called candyfloss," Wes explained, as the Star Boy studied the clouds of pink fluff spinning around inside a glass case.

"What is the purpose of 'candyfloss'?" he asked.

"You eat it, mate," growled the unsmiling bloke behind the counter.

"It is a *food* substance?" The Star Boy was clearly surprised.

"Yeah. So do you want some or not?" the unsmiling bloke asked.

"No, thank you," the Star Boy began to reply politely. "I do not consume human foo—"

"OK, let's go and find a ride you might like, Stan," said Wes, dragging him away from the stand, and following Kiki as she weaved through the crowds.

As they walked, Kiki pointed out the waltzers, the bumper cars, the high and twirling twisters and the rattling roller coaster.

"Why are the Humans screaming on some of the rides?" asked the Star Boy. "Are they frightened? Or in some way *enjoying* being so alarmed?"

Wes and Kiki both looked in the direction of the snaking carts of the roller coaster, as they hurtled downwards at high speed. Neither of them answered Stan's question straight away. Seeing the ride through his eyes, there were random bits of life on Earth that were unexpectedly tricky to explain.

"It's kind of both, really," Wes began to explain. "I know that sounds confus—"

"ACK-ACK-ACK!"

All three friends jumped as Harvey Wickes suddenly leaped out in front of them, his hands raised as if he was about to attack.

Wes felt his face flush pink.

"Got ya, Wesley No One!" Harvey bellowed directly at him.

"I – you – uh..." Wes bumbled, trying to find the right cutting words that – infuriatingly – wouldn't come.

Instead, he turned to check that the Star Boy was all right after Harvey's dumb alien impression. Wes noticed Stan titling his head this way and that, staring at Harvey the same way a bemused visitor at the zoo might study a snarling, laughing hyena.

"Come on." Kiki ushered both boys onwards. "Let's try and find something with no queue..."

"There!" the Star Boy announced, pointing at a carousel. A very *small* carousel.

"Stan, that's for little kids," Wes told him, looking at the slowly spinning and completely empty ride.

"But there is no queue, and I would like to experience it!" the Star Boy said, in total rapture at the mini merry-go-round. "Please?"

Two minutes later, Wes and Kiki watched the Star

Boy swirl past, waving from the pastel moped he was perched on, his feet on the pedals, his knees by his chest.

"I'm sorry if I sort of sprang this on you," said Wes, taking the chance to apologize. "It was just that Stan was so excited, and then, when I went round to get him, Eddie seemed to think Stan was doing all right with his energy today. And cos Eddie knows about technical stuff, I guessed it would be OK..."

"Just because Eddie can fix a hairdryer doesn't mean he's qualified to say that *Stan* is fixed!" said Kiki. "And anyway there's something I've been meaning to tell you. Eddie's asked me a couple of times about when Stan can move back to the basement at school. And that was *before* all the trouble yesterday!"

"What?!" said Wes, feeling uncomfortable curls of alarm in his chest. "Why didn't you say something earlier?"

"Well, I forgot BECAUSE of all the trouble that's happened since yesterday!" said Kiki defensively.

"So Eddie doesn't want Stan staying at the Emporium any more?" Wes checked, feeling slightly sick.

"Eddie didn't use those exact words. But he's definitely freaking out cos of all the glitches *and* how big his electricity bill will be with Stan using so much. I don't know how much longer he'll put up with it!"

"I hadn't thought about the extra cost of Stan recharging..." said Wes, alarm binding into a knot in his chest. "I suppose school is so big that the extra electricity he uses might not be noticed so much."

"Exactly. And the trouble is Stan's not going to be able to go back to the basement at Riverside for a long, *long* time, is—"

"Hello. I have completed the ride," Stan suddenly announced, appearing by their sides.

Wes hoped he hadn't heard any of that. He didn't want the Star Boy to get distressed about the situation. It was up to him and Kiki to figure something out – somehow.

"OK, so what do you fancy doing now?" Wes asked, slapping a cheery smile on his face.

"Can we go on the wheel in the sky?" the Star Boy suggested.

"The queue looks pretty big..." said Kiki, standing on tiptoe. "How about the ghost train? Doesn't look like we'd have to wait too long for that."

"Yes! This is the ride Ty mentioned," said the Star Boy.

Once they'd wended their way through the crowds and taken their place in the short but snaking line for the ride, Wes checked his phone, vaguely aware that Kiki was doing the same.

"I have no messages," the Star Boy announced, holding up his own mobile, having mimicked his friends. "What messages do *you* have?"

"One from my dad..." Kiki groaned, wrinkling her nose. "He and his girlfriend have arrived early. They're going to pick up my brother from school, then meet me here. I'd much rather stay with you two!"

"And I've got one from my dad saying he's sorry for not helping me with my homework this morning," said Wes, shoving his phone back in his pocket, as the queue shuffled forward. "I was kind of hoping it was Mum..."

Wes appreciated his dad's apology, but not the part of the message that he hadn't read out to his friends, asking him to come home straight away and not 'hang about on the streets'.

"Perhaps *I* can be of help with your homework?" asked the Star Boy eagerly.

Wes glanced over at Kiki, as they shuffled forward some more, getting closer to the entrance of the ride. Stan's enthusiastic offer suddenly made them both smile again.

"Actually, our homework project is called *Through Alien Eyes*, so you might be quite good at it," said Wes.

"Ah, yes!" exclaimed the Star Boy. "This is something Kiki suggested in class yesterday, before..."

The Star Boy trailed off. Wes wondered if his friend was experiencing a Human emotion. Guilt? Awkwardness? Regret?

"...before the incident," Wes jumped in, helping him out.

"Hey, let's not talk about that," said Kiki, glancing around to check who was in hearing distance. "Actually, keep your voices down... Lola and everyone are in the queue!"

"I will be excellent at this project!" the Star Boy babbled on, excited and unstoppable. "I am constantly trying to learn and understand how

Humans think and feel. For example, when I saw you talking with the Lola girl, Kiki, I saw her reveal a thoughtful side. But my guess is that she does not like to show weakness in front of her pack so she can remain their leader. It's behaviour seen in many wild animals, I believe?"

"Shh!" Kiki urged him, giving a little nod backwards to remind him how close Lola was.

"It's the same for the unpleasant boy called Harvey," the Star Boy carried on, lowering his voice only slightly. "He uses the technique of bullying to remain leader of *his* pack. He bullies everyone –"

"Tell me about it," muttered Wes.

"– *including* those who are his friends. They are afraid of him. I find this difficult to understand, as such behaviour is more usual in an enemy, I think?"

"I suppose it *is* hard for you to understand. I'm a human and I haven't a clue," muttered Kiki.

"So what else have you noticed about people, Stan?" asked Wes, trying not to raise his voice, though they were now very near to the entrance of the ride, and the WHOOOO!s and AAAARGGHHH!s from the speakers were starting to overpower their conversation.

"I have noticed that you and Kiki both very much dislike your parents," said the Star Boy.

"What?" Wes exclaimed.

"How can you say that, Stan?" said Kiki, sounding just as offended as Wes.

"Because you both complain about them," the Star Boy stated matter-of-factly.

"But ... but it's complicated," Wes bumbled. "I mean, I worry about my dad, and I get ... I dunno, disappointed by my mum."

Wes's head reeled. The trouble with the truth was it could hurt quite a lot.

"You see – these are negative words, I think?" the Star Boy pointed out. "So you *do* dislike your parents, the same as Kiki."

Wes felt his eyes prickle with unexpected tears. He suddenly felt too hot in his stupid jacket. He shoved the hood back off his head and undid the zip.

"Look, Stan, you don't understand!" he heard Kiki snap at their friend.

But before she could say anything more, a deely-bopper-headed young woman was herding the three of them quickly through the entrance, taking tokens from a fumbling-fingered Kiki and pointing at them to clamber quickly into a moving cart.

As soon as they sat down, Wes copied Kiki and pulled the safety bar down across their laps as they lurched off.

The WHOOOO!s and AAAARGGHHH!s roared louder in the darkness, as the three friends were suddenly hurtled at high speed towards a door that thwacked open into a chaotic, deafening version of space...

STAR BOY: The most terrible mistake?

The rational part of the Star Boy knew that he and his friends were inside a very crude illusion.

The black walls around the rattling, rollicking cart they were squashed together in, the ugly neon-painted space creatures that lurched and screamed at them ... they were made and decorated by the staff of the fairground, purely for amusement.

But, in that moment, the Star Boy felt dizzy with his surroundings. Or perhaps his head was just spinning and whirlpooling with worries.

In addition to his appearance on the school screens yesterday, he'd now caused his friends distress by stating facts about their parents. And, most crucially, he had just discovered that he'd been shockingly wrong about Eddie. The Star Boy had lip-read his friends' words as he walked over to them after completing several rotations of the mini merry-go-round. He was immediately distraught to realize that Eddie's friendly gestures this morning – the invitation to join him on the motorcycle ride, the gift of the brick phone – had masked the truth: Eddie wished him gone.

The Star Boy felt his head start to unspool and unreel, as if everything was coming undone. He didn't know if he could *ever* understand how Humans truly thought or behaved. Perhaps last night's Human-like 'dreamings' of the Absolute and the Education Zone were a way of showing him that the WORST mistake he had made was to think he could belong on this alien planet!

A searing rush suddenly flooded the Star Boy's system, pain jarring through his left hand. His head twirled and spun, overwhelmed by the dazzling spotlights that shone in his eyes ... the inescapable shrieking and wailing from the speakers ... and the monstrousness of the so-called alien creatures that lurched towards him, as if they would snatch him away!

The Star Boy opened his mouth and screamed, the sound more ear-piercing than anything blasting through the speakers.

WES: Seven words

"I thought it was the REAL alien in there for a minute!" someone burst out among the jabber of voices.

"Yeah, come to DESTROY us!" someone else laughed nervously.

"It's just a technical hitch, people; aliens are NOT allowed on our attractions!" joked the fairground worker, waving her torch and ushering everyone to follow her out of the broken-down ride. "Now if you can come this way, please..."

Wes blinked at the brightness as he stumbled into the weak sun of the late afternoon, along with Kiki and the Star Boy and the other stunned-yet-hyper passengers of the ghost train.

"You guys OK?" Wes asked. There'd been quite

a jolt when the emergency brakes came on, with everyone flying forward into the safety bars.

"I'm fine," said Kiki. "What about you, Stan? Was that another surge?"

"Yes," replied the Star Boy, looking tired and shaken. "I apologize sincerely for any alarm caused."

"That's all right, Stan," Wes said automatically.

"Well, it isn't all right at all, is it? " Kiki pointed out sharply. "Look, we need to get Stan back to Eddie's as quickly as—"

A trilling from Kiki's phone interrupted her sentence. Wes watched as she read the message on the screen and frowned.

"Uh-oh ... Dad's here in the park already, with Tasmin and Ty. Sorry, Wes, but can you get Stan home on your own?"

"Yes ... yes, of course!" Wes assured her.

"I'll call you both later," said Kiki, looking like she didn't want to leave, but hurrying off anyway.

Wes turned to the Star Boy, and noticed that he was rubbing his left arm.

"What's wrong?" he asked. "*Did* you hurt yourself on the ride just now?"

"No, I am uninjured," said the Star Boy, quickly

letting go of his arm. "Though I believe I will require recharging very—"

"Stop it! Stop it, ALL of you! It's NOT funny!" Wes suddenly heard a girl's voice yell from close by, rising high above a chorus of laughter.

It was Lola, Wes saw, but she wasn't exactly looking her normal, perfectly groomed self. Her cream furry jacket was soaked and stained brown where the now-empty bottle of cola she was still clutching must've tipped over her. There was also some kind of pink fuzz stuck to the jacket – as well as her hair and face. Wes spotted that she was holding a wooden candyfloss stick.

"It was scary in there, all right?" she yelled some more, as she threw down the bottle and stick and tried to peel off her drenched and messy jacket.

The girls that were supposed to be her friends were meanly pointing and laughing just as loudly as Harvey and his pals.

"I'm bored – let's go on something else," one of the girls was saying.

"C'mon ... leave her alone if she's in a mood," said a boy.

"Yeah, why don't you all just go!" Lola snarled,

as her so-called friends turned on their heels and sauntered off into the crowd.

"The unpleasant girl is shaking," Wes heard the Star Boy say. "I don't know if that is because she is angry or cold..."

Wes watched Lola fume and shiver, thinking she deserved to be treated badly by her friends just so she could experience how it felt to be on the receiving end of meanness. But, then again, Lola was looking pretty pitiful right now. He couldn't do much about the anger she was radiating, but he could do something about how cold she was.

"Hey, Lola," he said shyly, shuffling over and shaking off his jacket. "You can have this if you want?"

He expected her to bite his head off, but all the fight seemed to have seeped out of her. Standing a little taller than Wes, she looked at the padded jacket with mascara-smeared eyes, and wordlessly dropped her own ruined jacket on to the grass. Wes held out his Puffa, helping her wriggle into it.

"Thanks. Wow, it's really warm, isn't it?" said Lola, hugging the padded material round her.

"Yeah, and if you tuck your hair into the hood, no one will see how sticky it is," Wes suggested.

Lola stared at him for a second, then took his advice.

"You live across the road from me, right?" she said, quickly bundling her hair back.

"Yeah – I'm in the top-floor flat, above the dentist's," he answered, surprised that Lola had even registered his presence in the street.

"I'll drop this back to you later," she said, putting her hands in the pockets of the jacket and instantly pulling some random stuff out of them. "Do you need any of this?"

Wes looked at the clean but crumpled tissue, a grubby rubber, a lidless pen and a more-or-less empty asthma pump in Lola's hand.

Before he could get the chance to answer, Lola picked out the inhaler and offered it to him. He took it with a nod of thanks.

"But the rest is rubbish, right?" she asked, as she edged towards a nearby bin.

"Yeah, sure. You can dump all that," Wes said. "And don't worry about the jacket – it's too small for me. You can keep it – it suits you. Or, er, you know, bin it or whatever."

"It does look kind of cute on me…"

As Lola checked herself out, Wes bent down and scooped up the plastic bottle and wooden stick she'd discarded, as well as her own soggy jacket.

"Here..." he said, bundling up the jacket into a squashy sausage shape and handing it to her.

As Lola took it from him, someone lunged in between them.

"ACK-ACK-ACK!" roared Harvey.

Wes took a step back.

"OMG, give the alien stuff a rest! It's getting *so* boring!" said Lola, walloping Harvey with her rolled-up jacket. "Anyway I thought you lot had gone!"

"I just came back to check if you were bored of being in a huff with us and wanted to hang out again," said Harvey. "You *must* be desperate if you're talking to Wesley from the Planet Loser!"

Harvey reached over and roughly ruffled Wes's hair – and had his arm immediately whacked away by Lola.

"Ouch!" Harvey yelped. "What was that for?"

"Leave him alone. Wes is all right," Lola said sharply.

"Whatever," muttered Harvey, trying to sound like he didn't care, but moving away from Wes like a guard dog ordered off by its owner.

Wes blink-blinked, shocked to hear the seven little words Lola had just said. Seven words that meant a tiny but huge shift had just happened in his universe. Wes's one kind deed had made Lola see him differently. Instead of a no one, he was now a 3D person in her eyes. One that didn't deserve to be hassled by Harvey.

"Oh, hey!" she called out, as she began to walk away with Harvey. "Is this rubbish too?"

Lola held out her hand, palm up. Wes stared at the star earring, the silver sixpence, the smooth white shell ... the Mum mementos that he kept in his inside pocket.

"Yep, they're all rubbish," he said with barely any hesitation, and watched as Lola tipped the tiny treasures into the nearby bin.

"See you," she called out, disappearing into the crowds.

"See you," said Wes, even though she wasn't listening any more.

He turned to his friend, suddenly remembering the need to get Stan safely home.

But the Star Boy was nowhere to be seen.

KIKI: Playing at happy families

Stan and Wes should be back at Eddie's by now, Kiki thought to herself, as she sat cross-legged on the grass.

She was half-heartedly watching Ty goof around with Coco, holding on to her lead while running round in circles. Dad stood close by, laughing at the puppyish pair.

Behind them, music and excited roars rang out from the funfair rides. Tense as she was, Kiki couldn't help suddenly recalling a small something that had happened earlier when Harvey had done his annoying alien impression. She'd locked eyes with Lola for just a millisecond, with Lola doing a quick eye-roll, as if to say, "Isn't Harvey a total pain?" It was just a fragment of a moment, but one that felt like it might make a huge difference. Kiki and Lola would never be mates again. But if they could manage not to be enemies, how awesome would that be...?

"It's a lovely park," she heard Tasmin say, and turned round to see Dad's girlfriend kneeling beside her, smiling expectantly.

Kiki shrugged. "Yeah, it's all right."

In the last twenty minutes, Tasmin had described many random things as 'lovely': the town, Kiki's hair, the view of the nearby river, Ty's laugh...

This polite chit-chat is really annoying, thought Kiki.

And there were lots of irritating things about Tasmin, like the way she smiled ALL the time – it was really fake. And then there were her coloured glasses and the plastic clips in her hair (today's were strawberries). She was just trying way too hard to be cute. You'd never catch Mum dressing like that!

"So WHEN can we all go to the fair?" Kiki heard Ty suddenly ask. Her little brother had stopped running around and was now pointing in the direction of the music and the bright lights, while Coco tugged on her lead.

"Like your dad already said, Ty, we can't ALL go at once," said Tasmin. "It'll be too noisy and busy for the puppy!"

Great. So there was yet *another* annoying thing about Tasmin: she'd personally ruined their family tradition of going to the once-a-year fair. Well, Tasmin and the puppy.

"Yeah, it just didn't occur to us that puppies and crowded funfairs wouldn't mix!" said Dad with a laugh. "But here's what we'll do: me and you can go to the fair first, Ty, and Kiki and Tasmin can stay here with Coco. Then we can swap round. How about that?"

Dad's grin was as irritating as his stupid suggestion.

"Why don't we just leave Tasmin and Coco here?" Kiki jumped in, her temper up, her nostrils flaring. "Then me, you and Ty can go together, Dad?"

"Well, it wouldn't be very fair to leave Tasmin all on her—"

"NO, NO! COME BACK!" Kiki heard Ty yelp, and turned to see the puppy bounce off into a thicket of trees. "I didn't MEAN to let go of the lead, Dad! She just pulled REALLY hard all of a sudden!"

"Mike! Get her!" Tasmin shrieked. "COCO! Come back! COCO! STOP!"

"Don't panic! I'll sync with the tracker on her collar," said Dad, fumbling his phone out of his pocket while Kiki scrambled to her feet and followed the others in the direction of the disappearing dog.

STAR BOY: A kindred spirit

The Star Boy sat at the base of a tree, his body trembling as he attempted to reset his badly dysregulated system. From what had happened on the ghostly train, it was obvious that his surges were getting stronger, more unpredictable, more out-of-control.

And only minutes before – as he watched the unpleasant Lola girl throw away Wes's tiny treasures – he had felt himself teetering on the verge of a serious malfunction, as if he were about to Morph back to his true, alien self. In that frightening moment he'd taken the only course of action he could think of – he'd deserted Wes and run.

The Star Boy lifted his left hand, turning it this way and that, but there was nothing to see; no clues as to what was causing the prickling pings and pangs of discomfort, or more recently the acute shocks and stabs of chronic pain. Wiggling his Human fingers, he tried to push away a fear that had begun to fight its way into his consciousness. The fear that this *wasn't* an electrical energy imbalance problem; that it was perhaps a sign that he was becoming unwell... What would that mean for an alien on Earth? If the Star Boy started to deteriorate, what would happen? He could hardly turn up at the local hospital, begging for assistance.

Kiki's mother is a nurse. Perhaps, if I need urgent medical care, Jackie might help me? the Star Boy wondered, soothing himself with that possibility.

Bleep-bleep-BLEEP! Bleep-bleep-BLEEP!

The brick phone had made the same small noise many times in the last few minutes. He guessed it was Wes attempting to contact him. The Star Boy didn't answer, worried that in his still somewhat agitated state the phone might perhaps catch fire or explode. But in a moment, IF he managed to still himself, he would call his friend and reassure him of his whereabouts.

The shivering, frightened Star Boy closed his eyes, pushed his dark thoughts aside, and tried another of the quietening techniques Kiki's mother had taught him. Using the index finger of one hand, he ran up and down all the fingers of the other hand, as if he was drawing an outline. As he repeated the movement slowly back and forth, time and again, his pulses began to settle. He even managed to smile at the sensation – the tickling, Humans would call it.

And then something else tickled.

Unlike his finger, it was a wet sort of tickle.

The Star Boy opened his eyes and nearly screamed at the sight of the strange creature. It was very small, extremely hairy and appeared to be about to devour him with its tiny, shiny teeth and bright pink tongue.

Luckily, he managed to swallow down his panic, quickly identifying the strange creature as an infant canine. It looked very like the child dog he had seen with Kiki's father on the video call on Sunday.

"Are you in fact that same canine?" he asked the puppy, who responded by clambering on to the Star Boy's crossed legs and attempting to eat his face while wobbling its bottom end back and forth at an alarming rate.

"Are you allowed to be in the Outside by yourself?" the Star Boy asked. "Or are you lost?"

The animal's only communication involved staring up at him, as if it hoped he could help. Its eyes were as liquid black as his own. This creature was obviously an entirely different species to him, but there was comfort in spotting something so familiar.

"I was lost too," said the Star Boy, suddenly softening towards the mini-sized dog. "I think that maybe I still am..."

The dog booped its wet nose against his, for no apparent reason.

"You must have a family, I suppose," the Star Boy said to the pup. "You are very young ... do you still remember them? Do dogs miss their parents when they go to live elsewhere? Or are you more like me, with no memory of them?"

As soon as the Star Boy said that, the half-dreaming came to him again.

The day the Absolute visited the Education Zone. The presence by his side, the steady, reassuring voice in his ear, a calmness.

The Absolute was like a mother, a teacher and a ruler to everyone on his planet. Was the Star Boy 'remembering' her coming to see him in particular? But surely not; he would have an event so extraordinary logged in his data bank. He would have been able to play it, to view it in his lens at any point...

Trying to make sense of this current thought, the Star Boy absent-mindedly ran his hand over the plentiful fur of the dog, as he had witnessed Humans doing on YouTube videos he had accessed. It felt surprisingly warm, soft and pleasant. His fingers touched a piece of fabric fastened round the dog's neck, to which were attached three things:

- *a long red ribbon or rope*
- *a blue plastic orb, from which he could sense some electrical disturbance*
- *a silver tag with the word COCO carved upon it, along with several numbers.*

"So you ARE the same canine!" the Star Boy announced, remembering the name he had heard mentioned.

"COCO!" came a shout.

The Star Boy's quiet moment was no more, his

hideaway disturbed by a herd of who-knew-whats crashing through the undergrowth.

The small creature bounded off the Star Boy's lap, barking excitedly.

"Oh, thank goodness! Thank you for finding my puppy!" said a woman, grabbing the fluffy creature up into her arms.

"Hold on – were you trying to *take* our dog?" a man's accusing voice asked him.

"STAN! STAN!" yelped a young boy, who was most definitely, most wonderfully Ty.

"Dad – he didn't try and take the dog. This is my friend!" he heard Kiki say. "Stan, what are you doing here?"

"How did you find me?" the Star Boy blurted out, confused but pleased to see her.

"We didn't find *you*," said Kiki, helping him up. "We found the puppy. She has a tracker on her collar – that blue plastic thing? So Dad could pinpoint where she was on his phone..."

Kiki was pointing to the innocently tiny item, no bigger than a thumbnail.

But, as he noted it, the Star Boy's trio of hearts suddenly surged, and what felt like a heavy locked door at the back of his mind flew open. A flood of images rushed in and engulfed him.

A bright white room – that's what he could picture. A younger version of himself was sitting inside. This small Star Boy was gazing up at an Elder bent over him, telling him he was doing a good and important thing, that it would be all right. And then there was a short, sharp pain.

Now there were other Elders in the room, and the sound of pleased and celebratory chatter.

"Stan... Stan? Are you OK?" he heard Kiki ask.

The Star Boy nodded, his words quite lost to him as realization dawned.

What had just happened was not the result of studying images on his lens, or the dreamlike flickers of data he'd had in the night-time.

It was a memory.

A memory – the same as Humans had.

The Star Boy's pulses stuttered with shock as the memory came further into focus. The day the Absolute came ... she was to witness an experimental new programme taking place at the Education Zone. A selection of young Star Boys were the subject of the experiment.

He was one of those boys taken to the lab, told to take out his data lens, so he couldn't record what was happening.

They didn't want him to know what they'd done to him.

That they'd fitted him with a tracker.

All the surging and strangeness of the last few days, the pings, the pangs, the pain. It could only mean one thing.

He was being tracked.

They were coming to find him...

WES: A hoax and a hack?

Wes ran towards the waiting group of people by the trees, with Ty frantically windmilling his arms around to attract his attention.

"Hey, Wes! Look – Stan's here!" Kiki called out to him in as casual and carefree a voice as she could manage. He noticed that her eyes were wide with worry, though.

"Ah, great. OK," Wes panted, bending over and putting his hands on his knees to steady himself.

"Do you need to use your breathing device?" the Star Boy asked him with considerable concern.

"Got it – I'm good," said Wes, straightening up and taking a gulp of his inhaler.

"Asthmatic? Me too!" said the man, putting Wes instantly at ease. "We met briefly on FaceTime the other day, Wes. This is my partner, Tasmin."

"Hi," wheezed Wes, though his chest was already loosening.

"We lost our puppy and found Stan!" the woman said brightly.

"Uh-oh... Wes, have you seen the time?" said Kiki, pointing at her phone. "Didn't you say earlier that you and Stan needed to leave about now?"

That was code, obviously, and Wes understood it perfectly. Stan had a bad surge back at the fair. Stan had gone off on his own. Stan could potentially run out of energy soon, and if he did that, and started Morphing or glowing, then he – and his friends – would *really* be in trouble.

A buzzing jarred Wes out of his tangled thoughts. It was a text. Kiki and her dad were both checking out their phones too.

"It's from school," Wes mumbled. "**We are investigating an incident of the computer system being hacked. Apologies for any distress caused to students by this foolish hoax. Mrs Evans**"

Wes glanced over at Kiki, whose wide-eyed look had switched from fear to relief.

"What does your head teacher mean by 'distress

caused'?" said Dad, stating the obvious. "*What hoax?*"

"Before the power cut at our school yesterday, a person dressed up as an alien appeared on all the interactive screens," Kiki explained.

"Mrs Evans is basically saying that someone must've hacked into the school computer system," Wes added quickly.

Wes noticed that the Star Boy was staring from one face to another, assessing and absorbing the situation.

Wes hoped Stan understood that the head teacher was telling everyone – quite clearly – to stop fantasizing. There *was* no alien. Students could start laughing about the ridiculous idea of an actual space creature wandering the corridors of Riverside Academy and the streets of Fairfield.

"Right, Stan, we'd better get going," Wes said, quickly turning his attention to the here and now of getting Stan out of the park and hoping his smile told their secret alien everything he needed to know right now: the problems caused by yesterday's surges were over.

STAR BOY: Masking

All the way to Eddie's, Wes had insisted that the Star Boy was safe. That the alien in school had been explained away.

And, even though he'd nodded along to Wes's comforting words, the Star Boy felt as far from safe as he could imagine. But he didn't see any benefit in alarming his friend. What good would that do?

"Yeah? That's amazing!" Eddie enthused, as Wes perched on the arm of the sofa in the back room of the Emporium, telling him the 'good news'. "You must be so relieved, Stan!"

"I am very relieved," the Star Boy repeated automatically, smiling his mask of a smile, and reminding himself that this sanctuary was becoming more temporary by the hour. The incident at Riverside Academy might have had a welcome outcome, but his surges wouldn't stop. Which meant that Eddie might still ask the Star Boy to leave soon. Even more alarming was the possibility that the Elders would beat Eddie to it and snatch the Star Boy away, with no warning or chance of goodbyes.

"You look wiped out, though, Stan," Eddie commented. "You need to charge, right?"

"Yes..." said the Star Boy, gratefully sliding on to the floor, spreading his arms wide across the generator.

"Is he all right?" he heard Eddie ask Wes.

"I think so," Wes answered, sounding slightly uncertain.

I'm not all right. I have no sanctuary. I am not safe, thought the Star Boy as he began drifting into blankness.

KIKI: Like bubblegum about to burst

Teatime at Dad's Airbnb wasn't going so great.

For a start, it was weird finding out that the flat Dad had rented was in the same road as Lola's house, where Kiki had spent hours hanging out before she was un-friended. *Wes* lived somewhere in the street too, and it was particularly weird to think he was one of her new best friends and yet she had no clue at all where he lived.

But at the forefront of Kiki's mind right now was the fact that the flat wasn't exactly a relaxing space. The walls were paper-thin, and she could hear the grumpy *boom-boom* of a man's voice in the flat next door. Kiki couldn't make out what he was saying, but he seemed agitated. (She felt pretty agitated herself; the scare over an alien roaming round town might have turned into a joke, but that didn't solve the problem of the Star Boy's energy surges, or Eddie wanting him gone.)

And the puppy wasn't helping. It was barking at many, many things. The laces on Kiki's trainers. Its water bowl. The Cookie Monster on the front of Ty's T-shirt.

And when the puppy wasn't barking at things, it was biting them. Ty's joggers. The leg of the table. The leg of Kiki's chair. Kiki's ankles.

"Ow!" yelped Kiki, trying to shoo it away.

"Oh ... Coco doesn't mean to hurt you," Tasmin said earnestly. "She's just teething."

Without saying anything, Kiki leaned over to rub her ankle and spotted – too late – what the puppy was getting up to next.

"Oh no – Coco! *Stop!*" Tasmin suddenly called out, as the puppy crouched down and peed on the small backpack that Kiki had left on the floor.

"Hahaha!" sniggered Ty.

"*NOOOOO!*" groaned Kiki, putting her head in her hands.

"Calm down, Kiki!" said Dad, kneeling down to clear up the mess. "Coco's only a baby and the poor thing nearly got lost today!"

Kiki reeled at the unfairness of Dad having a go at her, however gently. If only he could look through her eyes, and see how hard all this playing-at-happy-families was. Cos he clearly didn't get it. He didn't realize that Kiki now felt like an outsider in her own family, replaced by a barky, bitey dog. Dad didn't understand that it was going to be beyond weird to have to visit him in a strange new home, where she'd feel more like a guest than a daughter.

Of course, Kiki couldn't say *any* of that, and so she snapped and said, "How could you let Tasmin give the dog that name!"

"What do you mean?" Dad said with a frown. "We named her together!"

Dad's reply only made her feel worse. As if he hadn't given Kiki a second thought once he and Tasmin got all loved up, especially now they had their furry dog baby.

"*Kiki* and *Coco*?" she said slowly and deliberately. "Do you realize how ridiculous that sounds, Dad? It's like the title of a kids' cartoon series..."

"I – I... It didn't even cross my mind," Dad said, fumbling around for his words.

"Mike, I *did* mention that it was a bit similar," Tasmin said softly, glancing up at him.

"Yes, but that's not the point," he said, trying to take charge of the conversation again. "Kiki, I don't think your attitude is exactly—"

"Mike..." Tasmin said, putting her hand on his.

She'd spotted the tears welling in Kiki's eyes. And now Dad did too.

"Oh, Kiki, no!" he said, coming to crouch by her side. "I didn't mean to upset you! Everything's got a bit muddled today, and I just wanted this visit to be perfect so—"

The hard thump and thud from the flat next door stopped Dad's explanation in its tracks.

And then came a new voice, a younger more desperate voice.

"Dad! *DAD!*"

Kiki froze, instantly recognizing it. She screeched back her chair and ran towards the door.

WES: Out of the blue

Wes came out of his steamy shower, pulled on his PJs, and walked straight into an ice-cold storm.

At least that's what the atmosphere in the living room felt like.

"What's wrong, Dad?" asked Wes, rubbing at his damp spikes of hair with a towel.

It had been a long, tricky day, but things had turned out OK-ish. No one in town was freaking out about aliens any more, thank goodness. And this afternoon Eddie had seemed pleased to see Stan. Had Kiki misunderstood what Eddie had said to her about wanting the Star Boy to leave soon?

"What's *wrong*?" Dad shot Wes's words back at him, all the while pacing back and forth across the carpet. "I'll tell you what's *wrong*, Wes – you keeping secrets from me!"

Wes froze, his mind immediately jumping to Stan.

"How do you think it felt having your mum ring me out of the blue just now?" Dad announced. "She said she tried to call you first –"

Wes gave himself no time to enjoy the fact that Stan wasn't the problem. Mainly because he was now picturing the phone tossed carelessly on the bed while he'd been in the shower, the call he'd missed.

"– but then she was straight on at me, demanding to know why you were calling her! She had immediately jumped to the conclusion that something was wrong. Started accusing me of not looking after you properly. As if SHE had any right to say that!"

Wes felt a hot flush of anger warm his face. From what Dad said, it sounded as if Mum had immediately picked a fight with him, which wasn't fair. But what also wasn't fair was Dad getting so angry with Wes for just wanting to speak to his own mother...

"I'm sorry, Dad. I'll call her back," Wes said quickly. "It's been a really long time and I just felt like having a chat with her. I'll tell her that everything's fine here."

Wes felt the weight of that last lie, as silence dropped like a stone between father and son, leaving only the faint sound of yap-yapping coming through the walls. Things weren't fine, not at all. They hadn't been fine in a long time.

"I wouldn't bother!" said Dad, his face suddenly as creased and crumpled as his shirt. "I told her if she thought *I* was doing such a terrible job, maybe you could move in with *her*! Well, *that* shut her up. Next thing she was saying how impossible that would be, with her *new* husband and her *new* kids and her *new* life…"

Wes felt any traces of happiness evaporate.

"Oh, for goodness' sake, I've had enough of that barking!" Dad roared, though his voice seemed oddly husky. "I mean, a dog? Someone's moved in with a *dog* next door?! Is that even legal in a second-floor flat? I can't handle that noise. I mean, if this goes on…"

Wes's father stumbled, suddenly unsteady on his feet, wheezing heavily.

"Dad – what's wrong?"

Before Wes's eyes, his father crumpled and fell, his head smacking the wooden floor.

"Dad! *DAD!*" yelled Wes, dropping down to his knees and trying to shake him awake.

With panic flooding his mind, Wes couldn't think what to do. As he continued to try and rouse his dad, the doorbell started ding-donging on repeat, and a muffled shout came from the other side of the door.

"Wes, WES! It's me – Kiki! Is everything all right in there?"

Wes couldn't think why his friend was on the other side of his front door, but he had never been so glad and grateful to hear her voice.

With shock turning him into a strange mix of stone and jelly, Wes let the adults pile in and take over. Kiki's dad and girlfriend both got down on the floor beside Dad, talking to him, asking if he could hear them, ringing for an ambulance.

"Can you take Coco, please, Kiki?" the woman asked, pushing the nosy, waggy-tailed pup away from her, as she gently turned Dad on his side, manoeuvring his arms and legs, like she was getting him into a yoga position.

"You OK?" Kiki asked Wes, as she tried to contain the flip-flopping, face-licking puppy in her arms.

"I don't know," Wes murmured numbly, as Ty's small hand slipped into his.

"It's fine – everything will be all right," Kiki's dad called over, the phone still pressed to his ear.

Wes's head felt foggy as he heard Kiki's dad continue to talk. Sometimes Mr Hamilton aimed questions at his girlfriend ("the operator says to check if he's breathing?" to which Tasmin thankfully said yes); sometimes his words were aimed at Wes ("they'll get an ambulance here as quickly as they can, but there'll be a bit of a wait...").

Then Wes instantly sharpened up when he saw the trickle of blood on the floor by his father's head.

"He's bleeding! It must have happened when he fell!" he blurted out.

"Don't panic, Wes," Tasmin said gently, as she crouched down to take a closer look. "The main thing is your dad's breathing well, and his pulse is good. Kiki, is Mum at home today?"

"Um, yes," Kiki replied. "Should I call her?"

"Absolutely," Tasmin said calmly. "Can you ask her to get here as soon as she can?"

Wes felt helpless as he looked down at his motionless but now gently moaning father. He had a huge urge to call someone himself. Someone who he knew would always be there for him.

Though quite what an alien boy could do right now to help, he had no idea.

STAR BOY: The joy of being needed

As soon as explanations were done with, Wes and Eddie had left the Star Boy to charge.

But once he was alone, and with the energy from the generator crackling and fizzing through him, the Star Boy frantically started the search.

First, he considered how small he'd been when the Absolute made her historic visit. That immediately helped him to estimate the period of data he needed to examine. Several Earth hours passed – the afternoon of Wednesday fading into early evening – before he found it. A short report with practically zero detail, but which answered everything.

The Absolute has announced that a promising tracking project has now been deleted after one

of the twenty units fitted exploded, causing
major damage to the volunteer.

The Star Boy didn't understand the use of that last word. It was an untruth. A lie. He had not volunteered to be fitted with a tracker, and he didn't suppose any of the Others had either. They were only what Humans would call little boys at the time. And which of the Others had been damaged? He had a vague sense of an empty seat in the classroom...

A great wave of anger swept over the Star Boy – but just as quickly he wondered if that was the wrong emotion. Should he perhaps be grateful? Wasn't the purpose of the trial to develop something that would keep the Star Boys safe in the future, if they became stranded, whether they wanted to be found or not?

Anger versus gratitude. The Star Boy didn't like having these conflicting feelings; this was a very Human way of reacting, which seemed pointless to him. *Certainty and practicality at all times*: he reminded himself of his planet's motto, hoping that might calm him and let him think more clearly.

It didn't.

"Hey, are you still asleep?" he heard Eddie ask, along with the clatter of the back door.

The Star Boy stayed still, eyes closed, feigning a blank period. He did not know what to say to Eddie at the moment, now that he knew he was causing his friend so much trouble and inconvenience. Now that he knew Eddie wished him to leave.

Though, of course, the matter of staying or leaving had no relevance any more, not if the rescue mission was on its way.

"OK, well, I'm just popping down to the chip shop," said Eddie. "But I'll be back in about twenty minutes."

• *chip shop – a takeaway food outlet that sells chunks of hot potato and fishes.*

As his data lens scrolled, the Star Boy heard the back door clatter shut again, releasing Eddie into the Outside. Now the Star Boy could rise and stretch and try and settle his thoughts.

And, once again, the cool of the yard might be a good place to start, he decided, leaving it a few minutes before heading out of the back door and feeling the gentle breeze skim his

Human-form skin.

For the last hour, he'd half listened as Eddie banged and crashed things around out here. Even though his head was crammed with confusion, a small smattering of curiosity rose in him. What had Eddie been doing? The Star Boy glanced around.

Visible in the yard was a washing line with two T-shirts, three pairs of boxer shorts and one sock dangling from it. Eddie's motorcycle and sidecar sat parked to one side. But there was also the small brick structure that the Star Boy had not paid much attention to before. A hodgepodge of boxes and containers and various metal bits and pieces was piled outside the open wooden door.

The Star Boy stepped through the door, peering inside the empty little structure. The space was cool and calm, with the last rays of the day's sunshine spilling through a little window. The Star Boy paused, watching the dust motes gently swirl in the light that was streaming through the unclean glass. They looked beautiful, reminding him of a star-dotted galaxy he'd once travelled through during an orienteering exercise. It made him feel a wave of what must be homesickness...

As he gazed round the small but serene space, the Star Boy became aware of a sensation in the pocket of his borrowed jeans. A vibration accompanied by a muffled jangling sound.

Grabbing the phone out of his pocket, the Star Boy stabbed at various buttons till one worked and he heard Wes's voice.

"Hello, Stan? Stan – can you hear me?"

"Yes! I can hear you, Wes!" said the Star Boy, straining to catch Wes's voice since he wasn't holding the phone close enough to his ear.

"Stan – my dad's hurt!"

"That is unhappy information. What is wrong with him?" asked the Star Boy.

"He's collapsed! He's barely conscious, and he banged his head when he fell," Wes answered, his voice sounding croaky. "But look – I need your help..."

"I will help in any way I can!" said the Star Boy, hurrying out of the empty shed.

"Kiki's mum's on her way over to yours. Can you ask Eddie to drive her here? She can look after Dad till an ambulance arrives. Kiki's trying to call Eddie, but he's not picking up..."

The Star Boy could hear the warble of a phone from inside the back room – it had to be Eddie's.

The truth was on the Star Boy's lips, ready to explain Eddie's absence. But he paused, wondering if it was an extremely opportune time to ignore the truth.

"Jackie will be transported to your home in the quickest time," he assured Wes.

"Great!" said Wes, sounding relieved. "Here's my address..."

The Star Boy stored the information on his data lens, immediately bringing up a map, coordinates and a route. He said goodbye to Wes, but his friend had already hung up.

Hurrying over to the open back door of the shop, he helped himself to two of the three motorcycle helmets piled on a shelf there ... the white one that Eddie had lent him the day before, as well as Eddie's own large red helmet.

Fixing Eddie's helmet on and pulling the visor down, the Star Boy clambered on to the motorcycle, while dropping the white helmet into the sidecar. Taking a deep breath, he concentrated all his energy...

The ignition crick-cricked, though no key was in it. The engine roared and sputtered into life, and the Star Boy beamed at his success, while examining the handles and the footrests and trying to remember how Eddie had operated this machine. Surely, having navigated a pod across the depths of space, the Star Boy could drive a very old Human vehicle along the high street, across the river and up to Wes's flat above the dentist's...?

"Oh great – you're ready, Eddie!" he heard Kiki's mum call out, as she rushed into the yard. "I'll take the sidecar..."

The Star Boy hesitated, wondering for a split second if he should admit the truth of who he was. But almost instantly he knew that his admission would waste precious time. And so he lowered his head and lifted his hand in hello, as Kiki's mum grabbed up the spare helmet and climbed into the little pod attached to the motorcycle.

"I tried calling and knocking at the front door just now, but—"

Her words were lost as the Star Boy raced out of the yard in a blaze of black smoke and revving.

As they hurtled off down the hill, the Star Boy felt

his energy soar, and he suddenly became certain of three things:

- *doing anything, anything to help the Humans who had helped him was his primary goal, in whatever time he had left before the rescue mission arrived*
- *he could have saved a lot of effort starting the motorcycle with the keys that dangled from the hook by the back door*
- *he had no idea what a 'dentist's' was and trying to scroll through data while driving an unreliable and rattling vehicle was probably not the wisest idea...*

"Oi! Hey!" came a yell, as they zipped past the chip shop on the high street.

The Star Boy glanced across at Kiki's mum and was grateful to see that she had her head down and was frantically texting, oblivious to the person who'd called out to them.

And as it was an emergency, the Star Boy could hardly stop. Instead, he simply waved to Eddie as he stood there holding his hot potato chippings and gawping.

Thursday: Time to say goodbye...?

STAR BOY: Unravelling

The dawn light was soft, brightness gently seeping into the darkness.

As the Star Boy walked invisibly across the dew-damp grass of the park, he marvelled as the fledgling sun glinted on the metal structures of the funfair in front of him, giving them a glow every bit as striking as when the electric bulbs illuminated them.

He passed the caravans where the fairground workers slept.

He drifted in the empty spaces between the stilled rides themselves, entrances padlocked shut, stalls curtained off.

Stopping at a bin, the Star Boy tilted his head this way and that. He recalled standing nearby with Wes, watching the unpleasant Lola girl hover at this very spot. For many minutes, he pulled out sticky and smelly food containers, carefully examining each one in turn, before laying them on the grass. Finally he was rewarded. The first of Wes's tiny treasures – the star earring – was in a drinks carton. The second – the silver sixpence – was stuck to a ketchup-covered serviette. The third – the shiny white shell – was at the very bottom of the bin, beside a half-eaten burger.

Clutching the objects in one hand, the Star Boy thought about Wes's casual words to Lola about them being simply rubbish. His friend had difficult feelings about his parents, but, just as Wes had been delighted to know last night that his father wasn't seriously ill (he'd had an occurrence known as a severe 'panic attack'), the Star Boy guessed Wes would be pleased to have his mother's treasures in his possession again, and he would enjoy returning them. It might be the last kind gesture he could do for his friend, if the rescue mission was on its way...

The Star Boy slumped at the thought of it, resigned to the fact that if they came for him there was no way to refuse. He should go back to Eddie's as quickly as he could, and contact his friends as soon as they were awake, to make the most of whatever time he had left.

But instead of leaving, the Star Boy stayed, the deserted funfair too mesmerizing to rush away from.

In front of him loomed the giant, turning wheel ride. He looked to the pod at the top of the wheel, and wished that yesterday he had been able to experience being up there, so very close to the sky.

Why not do it now? he suddenly thought.

Before he became more logical and changed his mind, the Star Boy vaulted over the locked gate, and scrambled into the nearest pod, which rocked gently as he settled into the padded seat.

Concentrating, focusing, he felt his energy rise and transfer into the engine that turned the huge structure, and was rewarded by the grind and groan of the mechanism coming to life, the vast circle beginning to turn.

The Star Boy knew the sound of it would stir the staff from their beds, but he suddenly didn't care. Everything was starting to crack apart.

As the pod slowly rose, he considered the mess he had made of things the previous evening. He had started out by doing a *right* thing – it was an emergency, and he had delivered Kiki's mother to Wes's flat very quickly, so that she might use her nursing skills on Wes's father.

But, at the same time, it had been a very *wrong* thing. Driving a vehicle when you're supposedly a child had caused much alarm to the adults.

And driving a vehicle when you don't understand what the red, green and yellow lights on poles mean could have been very dangerous, it turned out. At the flat, the wide-eyed stares of Wes, Kiki and Ty had made it clear to the Star Boy that his kind gesture had been very risky indeed. He'd quickly realized that if the adults hadn't been attending to Wes's father, they might have interrogated him further.

"This isn't over," Eddie had warned him once he'd collected the Star Boy and the borrowed motorcycle and taken them home to the safety of the Electrical Emporium. "Kiki's mum is going to be asking a *lot* of questions tomorrow, and I'm not sure how to answer them…"

The pod rose higher, lifting the Star Boy above the treetops. The town spread out all around, with the river drifting below, and birds drifting above, in the peach-and-pink tinted sky. The view of all this and of the jagged jumble of rooftops and distant green fields and wooded hills made his stilled hearts nearly pound with joy.

But it's probably best that I go soon, the Star Boy thought sadly.

He was all too aware of causing complications for his friends, who had the impossible job of hiding him and explaining him and trying to teach him to be Human.

And he knew he was struggling to get things right, to understand what being Human was about. Perhaps he was better suited to being back on his own planet, where strict rules and routines laid down by the Absolute meant there was no room for confusion.

The Star Boy was at the very top of the wheel now, staring up into the sky that was slowly blooming into blue. It was so strange to think of the inky darkness of space beyond. So strange to think of the spacecraft that was quite possibly hurtling towards him right now.

How will the rescue happen? he wondered,

imagining the Star Men beaming down into the backyard of the Emporium in the middle of the night, sliding the door open, gathering round him as he lay by the generator and leading him away...

And then his wondering abruptly ended with a jab of excruciating pain in his left hand. The Star Boy cried out, at the same time hearing the voices below of staff running to the ride to see what had malfunctioned.

Glancing down at his hand, the Star Boy initially saw nothing – it was as invisible as the rest of him. But clutched in his palm were the silver and white of Wes's treasures, and along with them a red dot glowed, pulsing ominously.

With a shudder of dread, he guessed what it was: the red dot of a tracker ... the source of all the pain, all this time, as it began to activate.

Staring at that small, fiercely glowing red dot, the Star Boy felt a wrench of fear.

Bizarre and complicated and frustrating as Humans were, how could he leave his Kiki and Wes, his Eddie and Ty? How could he leave this planet when there were so many earthly marvels to witness?

His data lens whirled as he recalled locations

he'd learned about in the Education Zone:

- *Kaikōura in New Zealand, where entire schools of whales arced in slow motion from the swelling waves*
- *Namibia in Africa, where sprawling herds of unicorn-antlered oryx trekked through the endless rolling pink sand dunes of the Namib Desert*
- *Wulingyuan in China, with its stone forest of dizzyingly high rock pillars, jagged tips piercing passing clouds*
- *Siquijor in the Philippines, where – when darkness fell – the beaches and waterfalls were lit by the eerie glow of swirling swarms of twinkling fireflies...*

The Star Boy wanted to witness ALL of these wonders and more for himself.

But most of all, right now, he wanted to be in the cosy kitchen of a small flat in Fairfield – and ask one particular person to save him.

WES: To be OK, or not to be OK

At first, Wes thought that the fluttering sensation on his face was just another of the many strange dreams that had buffeted about in his head all night.

But then he heard Kiki's voice, and remembered where he was. Instead of his own bed, he was on an inflatable mattress on the floor of Ty's room.

"Ty, get that hamster off Wes!" Kiki ordered her brother.

"AWWW..." he heard Ty groan, and then the clank of what sounded like a cage door opening and closing.

Wes pushed himself on to his elbows, just as Kiki settled herself on the other end of the mattress, bouncing him upright. It felt funny-peculiar to be hanging out with his friend, in her flat.

"Did you sleep all right?" Kiki asked, her curls loose and boinging like a beautifully dark cloud.

He was just about to answer with a half-hearted "sort of" when Kiki's mum put her head round the door.

"I've made pancakes and hot chocolate... They're on the kitchen table waiting for you all!"

"YAY!" yelled Ty, zipping off in his dinosaur pyjamas.

"And I've got some good news for you, Wes," said Kiki's mum, still leaning on the door frame as Wes tried to get up off the squeaky mattress as quietly as he could. "I just called the hospital and they told me your dad slept well after his X-ray and stitches. And they've just checked all his vitals again – it definitely was just a severe panic attack that caused him to collapse."

"*MUUUUMMMMM!*" they heard Ty yell.

"We'll be there in a minute!" Kiki's mother called back. "Help yourself!"

"So does that mean he's coming home today?" asked Wes, feeling happy, feeling anxious, wondering just how well his dad would actually be.

Kiki's mum seemed to spot that in his face.

"Yes, he'll be discharged today, Wes, but he's going to be seen by a specialist doctor first, someone who'll talk to him about what's going on. I think your dad might be finding life a bit tough."

Wes knew it was true, but it hurt to hear.

"*MUUUUMMMM!*"

"We're coming, Ty!" Mum called back. "But look, please see this as something positive, Wes. Last night might have been scary, but it's the start of your dad getting the help he needs. This will be really good for both of you."

"I knew things were getting worse, but I didn't know what to do," said Wes, letting himself feel a flicker of hope at what Kiki's mum had just said.

"Of course you didn't!" she said with a warm smile. "You're a kid!"

"I feel bad that I get cross with him sometimes..." Wes muttered.

"I get cross with my dad too," Kiki said, trying to make him feel better. "*And* my mum!"

"Yes, you do!" said Kiki's mum with a wide grin. "And listen, feelings can be complicated. You can be annoyed with someone and still love them. Or love someone and be annoyed with them. That is absolutely allowed. And one *more* thing you should know, Wes: adults don't *always* get it right. We're not perfect – at all!"

Wes blink-blinked, taking in what he'd just heard. It felt good. It felt like he could breathe a bit easier.

"*MUUUUUMMMM!*"

"Come on, we'd better go and see what your brother wants – and check he's not eaten ALL the pancakes..." said Kiki's mum, heading back down the hall.

"I really think it'll be OK," Kiki murmured, putting her arm round Wes's shoulder and giving it a squeeze as they followed after her mum in their bare feet. But as soon as they got to the kitchen Wes wasn't so sure.

Because sitting at the table next to Ty was a glowing amber boy.

"Jackie, help me, please..." said the Star Boy.

KIKI: A duty to help

"What ... what *is* that?" Kiki's mum blurted out as she stared at the glowing entity in her kitchen. "How did it get here?"

"Well, I let him in, of COURSE!" said Ty, squeezing half a bottle of maple syrup on to his plate. "He knocked at the kitchen window and cos he's our friend I invited him in."

"Please don't be alarmed, Jackie!" said the Star Boy.

"What? How do you know my name? I – I don't understand," said Mum, backing away from the table. "Ty, come over to me, baby. Quickly!"

"But why?" said Ty, stuffing a piece of pancake in his mouth. "It's JUST Stan. He LOOKS like this sometimes."

"I do," the Star Boy agreed. "But I am the same boy you know."

"Ty! *Please* come here!" Mum ordered Kiki's brother.

"Look – Ty's right, Mum. Please don't panic," Kiki implored her mother. "*Please* just let us explain."

Kiki glanced over at Wes for support, and took a short but deep breath.

"This is going to be hard to believe but please listen. Me and Wes found Stan at school."

"We did, Mrs Hamilton!" Wes chipped in.

"Stan's actually ... well, he's an alien," Kiki continued. "He got stranded here and he's been staying with Eddie."

"Eddie...?" was all Mum could say, though it was pretty obvious that her head was jumbled with a thousand urgent questions.

"Yeah, and Eddie's coming NOW," announced Ty, standing up and pointing out of the kitchen window, where their friend could be seen running across the road. "I called him on your phone, Mum. To tell him Stan was here, in case he thought he was LOST."

"Hi! Hello!" Eddie called out, barging in without

bothering to knock or ring the doorbell.

"Eddie, what's happening here?" asked Mum, looking from Eddie, to Kiki, to Wes, to Ty ... and to the Star Boy, where her shocked gaze stayed.

"Jackie – sorry, I know this must be freaking you out. But it's all OK. Really," Eddie tried to reassure her.

"How ... I mean, when..." Mum bumbled, unable to shape her thoughts into sentences.

But Kiki was suddenly more concerned with the Star Boy. Appearing here as his natural glowing alien self – didn't that mean something *had* to be wrong?

"What's going on, Stan?" she asked, sitting on a chair beside him.

"Kiki!" Mum gasped.

"Mum, shush," said Kiki, holding her hand up. "You don't know enough about Stan yet. *We* do."

"What is it, Stan? Why haven't you Morphed into a human boy?" said Wes, stumbling into the last free chair around the table. "Are you hurt? Has something happened?"

"I have no more energy to hide or to fight. There is no point," the Star Boy stated. "They are coming for me, and I don't want to go."

"What?" Kiki and Wes yelped in unison.

"*NOOOO!*" squealed Ty, jumping out of his seat to hug the Star Boy.

Mum automatically went to grab Ty, but Eddie put a hand on her arm, to try and show her that Ty was in no danger.

"How can they be coming for you?" Eddie asked. "Your classmates blew up your pod in the playground last week. They think you're dead!"

"What...?" Mum gasped, her eyes like saucers. "There were *other* aliens here in Fairfield?"

"I think it is a rescue mission," said the Star Boy.

"What? I don't understand!" Mum blurted out. "What is it saying?"

"Mum – honestly, I do love you, but *please* be quiet for a sec," said Kiki. "Cross my heart, we'll explain everything later. Just let Stan talk for now."

Stunned, Mum fell silent, holding the back of Ty's chair to keep herself steady.

"How do your people know where to find you, Stan?" asked Wes.

"I have discovered that they fitted a tracker in me," said the Star Boy, showing them all the red dot of light in his hand. "I was very young. I didn't remember the experiment till yesterday…"

Kiki, Wes and Ty leaned closer to see the tiny pulsing shape.

"It's why I've been experiencing so many surges. They must have been attempting to home in on me," the Star Boy continued. "And, now that this tracker is activated, I assume they are on their way. It will not take long for them to reach me."

"How long is not long?" asked Kiki.

"A few hours at the most," the Star Boy guessed. "But I'm not familiar with this technology, and they *could* be almost here."

"BUT YOU CAN'T LET THEM TAKE YOU AWAY!" wailed Ty. "MUM, DO SOMETHING!"

"What? Ty, what on earth can I do?!" said Mum, incredulous at the situation unfolding in her kitchen.

Kiki saw the Star Boy look imploringly at her with his huge black eyes, lids closing from side to side.

"Jackie, you are a nurse," he said. "Please will you cut the tracker out of my hand?"

Kiki turned to her mum. "Yes! That's brilliant – please, Mum. Do it now!"

"But I can't!" said Mum. "I mean, I *do* have a

surgical blade here, but I don't know how much you would bleed –"

"I do not have any blood," the Star Boy informed her.

"– then there's your muscles and ligaments. I don't know their position," Mum carried on protesting.

"I have neither of those," said the Star Boy.

"But your skin – I can't even see where I'd make the incision…" Mum continued with her protests.

"Perhaps this will help?" said the Star Boy, slowly Morphing from his amber glow to his Human form.

"Oh!" gasped Mum.

"HAHAHA!" Ty sniggered. "Stan, you have no clothes on. AT ALL!"

"Here," said Kiki, wriggling out of her dressing gown and passing it over to the Star Boy to wrap himself up in.

"Please?" said the Star Boy, offering his more recognizable hand to Mum.

"Mum – you're a nurse! It's your duty to help people in need, whoever they are!" said Kiki.

Her words seemed to get through.

"I might not understand *any* of this…" she said, giving herself a shake, and sounding more like the capable person she was, "but OK, let's do it. I'll look out the blade and the sterilizing solution. Kiki, get a dressing out of the first-aid box. Wes, help your friend to wash his hand thoroughly. Ty, find my glasses."

"And, if you manage to remove the tracker, I'll blitz it with my soldering iron," said Eddie, as excited by the new plan as Kiki, Wes and Ty clearly were. Before anyone could comment, he ran out of the flat to fetch it.

"Thank you, Jackie," said the Star Boy, looking at Mum with an expression of adoration.

"You're welcome, er ... Stan," said Mum, pausing at the kitchen doorway.

If Mum wasn't in such a hurry, what with performing minor surgery on an unexpected alien, Kiki would have given her the BIGGEST hug.

STAR BOY: No more alien eyes

The Star Boy in his bare feet and scruffy towelling dressing gown.

Kiki in her pyjamas of T-shirt and shorts, yellow flip-flops slapping on the paving stones, too full of adrenalin to feel the cold.

Wes in his Star Wars PJs, with a hoodie and trainers quickly shoved on.

The three of them pelted down the hill, sprinting across the high street and down the lane that took them to the river. Eyes followed them as they ran, people pointing and smiling, wondering what the occasion was.

"Maybe they think we're doing it for a dare!" Kiki breathlessly suggested.

The Star Boy didn't waste time sourcing the

meaning of 'dare' on his data lens. He was too elated with the present task.

"Who cares?" Wes laughed, as he led the way on to the pedestrian bridge.

They all stopped in the middle, the Human pair panting, the Star Boy's pulses pounding.

"Ready?" said Kiki, smiling at the Star Boy.

"Yes!" he said, holding his left hand up, and marvelling at the white padded dressing upon it, like a badge of freedom.

"HOLD ON! WAIT FOR US!" Ty called out, as he ran to join them, his hand in Eddie's.

The Star Boy halted, though he was itching to do this final stage. With the tracker cut out, and the bright red bead burned till it shrivelled, darkened and died, it was time to let it go.

"OK, NOW you can do it!" said Ty, as Eddie lifted him up into his arms to see better.

Without another moment's hesitation, the Star Boy opened his fist and let the tiny speck fall. Such an insignificant-looking thing, like a blackened grain of rice... It was so incredible to think it had almost been powerful enough to change his life. And yet it had in a way. Just not the way it was intended.

"It's gone. Good riddance," said Kiki, as the wizened tracker disappeared into the choppy waves of the Wouze.

"You can just be a NORMAL human boy now!" said Wes. "Well, a *nearly* normal one for now!"

"Yes. But I will still need to find a permanent home," said the Star Boy, turning to look shyly at Eddie. "I know I am a burden to you…"

Eddie turned to him with a startled look on his face, and let Ty slide to the ground again.

"It's true, I did feel that at first, Stan, but I've got kind of used to having you around," said Eddie, grinning now. "I like the company. Even if you make things a bit complicated!"

"That's like ME!" announced Ty, swinging off Eddie's arm.

"Yeah, I guess!" laughed Eddie, looking down fondly at Kiki's little brother.

The Star Boy noted Kiki's look of surprise. Wes wore the same expression too. Like him, his friends were clearly startled at Eddie's change of heart.

"But, Eddie, only a few days ago, you told me you were worried about Stan causing trouble with the shops next door," said Kiki.

"Oh, Mrs Crosby and Mr Pickle totally trust me – I can always sort things out with them," Eddie said with an easy-going shrug. "Plus Stan's energy is *bound* to be much more settled now that tracker's not interfering with his system, so there hopefully won't be any more glitches and surges."

"But there is the issue of me absorbing much of the power of your home," the Star Boy reminded him.

"True ... but listen – do you understand the principle of car batteries charging when you drive?" Eddie asked.

The Star Boy had studied the principles of automation in Human vehicles. It came up in Earth Studies in the Education Zone one term. He quickly scrolled through his data, recalling the relevant information.

"There is a chemical reaction within the battery that is a catalyst, which produces electrons. The electrons generate electricity," he said aloud.

"Exactly. But did you notice something happening when you were on the motorbike yesterday, Stan?" Eddie asked, and got a puzzled look in return. "Did you feel yourself absorbing those electrons, in the same way you do with the generator in the back room?"

"I – I think that is true!" the Star Boy said in surprise. "I did indeed feel very energized when we returned from the trip."

"And you didn't need to use the generator when we came back," Eddie pointed out.

"Yes! I only used it after the drain on my energy from the incident on the ghostly train," the Star Boy remembered.

"Exactly. So I'm thinking that if you come for a ride with me every day, Stan –"

"Dropping ME at school!" Ty butted in.

"– *that* might be enough to keep you going, without relying on the generator!" said Eddie. "Just *no* driving the motorbike yourself!"

The Star Boy, Kiki and Wes all smiled at Eddie's teasing, and smiled even wider as the way forward became clearer.

"And hey, I started clearing out the shed in the yard for you yesterday, Stan," Eddie continued. "I know you like the coolness of outdoors. It was going to be a surprise... I've looked out an old armchair and a set of shelves you could store things on."

"It will be like a small home just for me?" the Star Boy said in awe.

"Sure!" said Eddie brightly, pleased that his surprise had gone down so well. "And I thought we could get you your own fairy lights, so it's cosy."

The Star Boy's hearts pounded with happiness.

"Thank you, Eddie," he said.

"No worries," said Eddie, grabbing a wriggly Ty into a friendly bear hug. "But, if you're here for good, we have to think of ourselves as a team. And that means figuring stuff out together."

So stunned, so pleased in the moment, the Star Boy had no words. Till he remembered something he DID have.

"Wes, I retrieved these for you," he said, opening his right hand and letting the tiny treasures trickle into Wes's upturned palm.

"Wow..." muttered Wes. "I – I'm ... thank you, Stan. I guess I should try and call my mum again. Tell her about Dad."

"When I was waiting in the kitchen this morning, I heard Kiki's mother talk to you about adults not always getting things right," the Star Boy said to Wes. "Your own mother is perhaps good at getting things wrong, I think? But I think you are allowed to tell her the truth of that. And still love her."

Wes smiled and lifted his shoulders. "I'll try. I'm working on being braver," he replied.

"And Kiki, perhaps you must find a way to be more content with your father and the friend of his who is a girl."

"*Girlfriend*," Kiki corrected him. "And I don't know if I'm pleased you're staying now, Stan – not if you're going to be lecturing us all the time!"

She was joking – the Star Boy saw that from her smile.

"But yeah, I suppose we do need to have a talk, just me and Dad," said Kiki. "And I guess Tasmin's OK really. I might go and buy some dog treats from the pet shop before we meet up with her and Dad and Coco later..."

"Dog treats? Would I like these?" asked the Star Boy, ready to learn more, more, more about *everything* on Earth as fast as he possibly could.

"*YES!*" yelped Ty, laughing himself stupid.

"NO!" shouted everyone else.

As they all turned and began to head back the way they'd come, the Star Boy took a moment to look over in the direction of the park, where the giant wheel rose up above the green tips of the trees. The blue sky above it had wispy drifts of clouds lazily moving across it.

He gave a little shudder. And shuddered again as he thought that the failure to track him would undoubtedly be discussed among the highest level of scientists on his planet. And with the Absolute herself, obviously.

But the Star Boy needed to leave thoughts of his old planet and people behind. He was now undoubtedly and wonderfully an inhabitant of *this* world. He'd work on no longer seeing the Earth through his own alien eyes. With the help and teaching of Kiki and Wes, he would continue to shape himself into the best sort of Human he could be.

And, in addition to the friends (family?) he'd been so lucky to find, he had a new ruler to look up to, to be advised by, to belong to.

The Star Boy couldn't wait to hear more words of wisdom from his latest rescuer, his new Absolute, Kiki's mum Jackie.

Jackie ... her name itself was like the music of

a ukulele, as beautiful as any pigeon in flight, as radiant as the fat coloured bulbs at the fairground, as—

"Oi!" shouted Kiki. "Get a move on, Stan!"

The Star Boy smiled, giving a quick wave goodbye in the direction of the sky, before doing as Kiki advised and getting a move on, into his new life.

**Discover how the
Star Boy's life on Earth
began in *How To Be A Human*.
Turn the page to read an
extract...**

The first storm

It came out of nowhere.

On the TV news, the cheery weather forecaster had predicted a fine, clear October night. But in the deep dark of the early hours, fierce cracks of thunder broke out – like granite cliffs exploding – and in rolled the storm. It startled the townspeople of Fairfield awake and sent them scurrying to their windows to see what was going on. In the brief hollows between booms, lightning fizzed and crackled and scarred the sky. The stars twinkled and twitched, blinking with the shock of it all.

House by house, flat by flat, lights and lamps flicked on till – *snap!* – the power cut plunged every building into darkness. The inhabitants bumbled about, searching for torches and candles, all clueless about what the town's river was getting up to. The meandering Wouze had suddenly swelled to twice its size and did what it had never done in its entire history ... went walkabout. Up, up, up it soared, spilling over its banks, gliding across pavements and merrily gushing along roads. It seemed to want to know what the inside of buildings and houses looked like, sluicing through tiny gaps under locked front doors.

Then, as suddenly as it had started, the storm stopped, leaving the expanded river stranded. In that moment of calm, the power flicked back on, letting the stunned population of Fairfield get a good long look at the damage that had been done by the unexpectedly wild weather.

Outside, tree branches and For Sale signs swam alongside each other in newly formed streams.

Inside, occupants sloshed around in knee-high water, trying to rescue precious things, while pyjamaed teens and kids wowed in wonder at their river-soaked homes.

And far, far away – streaming through space – someone felt VERY guilty about what had just happened.

The damage next day

KIKI: Fame and shame

Kiki's eyes flicked from the new posts on her phone to the breakfast news on TV. But it was still just some presenter blah-blahing about politicians arguing with each other. Nothing yet about the completely nuts weather in Fairfield last night.

"I'm not sure what time I'll be home from the hospital, Kiki," Mum called out from the hall, as she packed her nurse's uniform into her bag. "There's bound to be a staff shortage today with so many roads cut off."

"Hmm?" mumbled Kiki, all curled up on the sofa. In her lap was the TV remote, a plate of peanut butter on toast and her mobile.

She scrolled past an image of the usually neatly clipped grass of the park, which was now a shallow lake. It was lucky that her family's ground-floor flat was a little uphill, on the north side of town, so they'd escaped the worst of the weather madness. The torrential rain *had* slithered under the wafer-thin gap at the bottom of their front door, though, so that when Kiki first got up, the carpet had felt like spongy, boggy moss to bare toes.

"I said I'm not sure what time I'll get home!" Mum called out again.

Kiki heard her this time but was too busy scanning Snapchat for her schoolmates' storm stories to give a reply. Her best friends, Lola, Zainab and Saffron, all lived on the flatter south side of the river, close to school. Lola had just posted a pic of her living room, with water lapping at the bottom of her mega-screen TV and her sliders bobbing about like mini dinghies.

Zainab's post was of her excited little sister splashing about in the mud-coloured paddling pool that their kitchen floor had become.

Saffron messaged to say that she'd heard Harvey Wickes's gran had bodyboarded out of the front door of her flooded cottage, using a plastic sledge she'd dragged down from the loft.

(Disappointingly, there were no photos of that…)

"Kiki! Are you listening to me?" Mum asked, appearing in the doorway, jangling her door keys in her hand.

"Mmm, yeah … I'm listening," Kiki muttered.

"Not sure if I'm entirely convinced by that," Mum said with a sigh, as she disappeared back into the hall. "But one more thing: Eddie's not opening his shop today, so he's going to stick around and help out here, which is handy, considering both your schools are shut."

Kiki rolled her eyes. Her six-year-old brother Ty was annoying enough – having Eddie as a sort of part-time nanny was like having an annoying big brother too. Eddie might be twenty years older than Ty, and have a qualification in electronics, but he was easily as goofy. He helped Mum out by looking after Ty a few days a week when she had long shifts. He shut up his repair shop early on those days and picked up Ty from school on a spluttering, ancient motorbike with a clattering sidecar, the two of them looking like something out of a kids' cartoon in their matching red crash helmets. It was mortifying.

"They should be back soon," Mum carried on.

"Unless they've drowned..." Kiki said under her breath.

Bright and super early this morning, Eddie had come knocking to suggest that he and Ty go and splosh round town in their wellies. It suited Kiki if they took their time; she was looking forward to having the flat to herself once Mum left for work, even just for a little while.

Settling herself even deeper into the comfy sofa, Kiki stared at her mobile – speeding through more storm-related posts – till her attention was snagged by the mention of a familiar name on the television.

"...in Fairfield, where a completely unexpected storm last night caused never-before-seen flooding in the town," said the newscaster, his silver-grey eyebrows bent into curls of concern as he sat in the comfort of the warm, dry studio. Behind his head was an inset image of Fairfield's ornate town hall, which was just a few minutes down the hill from Kiki's flat. The town hall's grand steps led on to what looked more like a harbour than a high street.

"Whoa..." mumbled Kiki, jerking to attention.

Without thinking, she put a foot on the floor and instantly winced as the wetness of the carpet seeped uncomfortably through her sock.

"Mum! Mum, come QUICK!" she yelled, at the same time trying to rescue the contents of her lap as the remote control, toast and mobile slipped sideways. "Fairfield's on the news – we're famous!"

"Really?" said Mum, reappearing in a flash. "What are they saying?"

Kiki waved her arms wildly to shush her.

"Our reporter, Lisa Garcia, is in Fairfield now," the newsreader continued. "Lisa, can you tell us more about this unprecedented incident?"

"Yes, thanks, John," said the young female reporter, who now filled the screen. "You may think I'm standing in the middle of a river, but it is in fact the town's main street."

Kiki noticed that Lisa Garcia looked nervous. Then she spotted the problem: little waves of floodwater were slapping and slurping over the top of the reporter's red wellies.

"There's not a soul in sight here, John. Clearly, everyone is busy trying to deal with the catastrophe that hit their homes in the early hours," Lisa carried on professionally. "Except, hello ... I've just spotted someone! Hi, there!"

The reporter beckoned someone off camera to come closer. From the left, a boy awkwardly sploshed towards her, his knees playing peek-a-boo in the gap between his skater shorts and wellies. Even though it had stopped raining, the boy had the hood of his black Puffa jacket pulled up. A tuft of white-blond hair peeked out from under it, above his round pale face.

"Can I ask your name?" said Lisa, flipping the microphone towards the boy.

"Wes," said the boy, blinking madly as he leaned in too close to the mic.

"So is your school shut today, Wes? Has it been badly flooded?"

Lisa tried to move the mic away so he wouldn't foghorn into it again, but the boy just leaned closer.

"Yes," he said, peeking out of the hood.

Lisa hesitated for a second, hoping for more, before realizing she wasn't going to get it.

"And what's the name of your school?"

"Riverside Academy."

"Ooh, he's from Riverside!" said Mum. "Do you know him, Kiki?"

"He's in my year, but I don't really *know*

him," Kiki replied, flapping her arms again to shut Mum up.

Kiki didn't really know many of the other Year Sevens. She and her old primary-school friends, Vic and Megan, didn't even speak to each other any more. Within a week of starting at Riverside, Kiki had found herself scooped up by the Popular Crew. That didn't go down too well with Vic and Megan, and when they'd overheard Kiki describing them as "just some girls" she "sort of knew" from primary school, it had been the final straw. Vic and Megan had never forgiven her and had found a new crowd to hang out with. Kiki could hardly blame them. She'd have done the same if it was the other way round.

But as she stared at the boy, Kiki realized she *had* noticed him around in the corridors, constantly blinking or drumming his fingers on some book or other, and always, *always* being shouted at by passing teachers to take his hood down and "get that jacket off".

"The storm was short but savage." Lisa persevered with her interview. "It must have been pretty terrifying to witness?"

"Er, not really," said the boy. "I was watching *Star Trek Beyond* on my laptop and fell asleep with my headphones on. So I missed it."

Kiki burst out laughing, then started frantically messaging Lola, Zainab and Saffron.

Switch on the news – you have GOT to see who they're interviewing from our school... #TOTALGEEKALERT!

She paused for a second, wondering if the hashtag was too mean. But then it was the sort of thing Lola would say, so surely that made it OK, didn't it?

"EXCUSE ME!" came a high-pitched yelp from the TV. "*I* saw what happened!"

"Oh my goodness, Kiki!" gasped Mum. "It's your brother – it's Tyreke!"

Kiki looked up at the screen again.

Both Lisa and the hooded boy had swivelled round. They were staring at a young boy behind them. He was floating past the town-hall steps on an inflatable flamingo, wearing a red crash helmet and waving a lightsabre.

"It was ALIENS! I watched them out of my bedroom window!" Ty shouted.

"Oh no," mumbled Mum, slapping her hands to her face. "Not *this* again..."

"They were zooming around in SPACESHIPS that were like GLOWING DODGEMS doing LASER QUEST!" blurted Ty.

"Noooo!" groaned Kiki.

Kiki's brother was an expert fibber. His lies were legendary. All his friends still stared down at Kiki's feet whenever they saw her, even though she'd *twice* taken off her trainer and SHOWN them that she didn't have an extra toe. And the trusting little gang absolutely believed that Ty's part-time childminder, Eddie, had a secret government lab in the back of his dilapidated electrical repair shop, when all Eddie *actually* did was fix people's toasters.

As for Mum, her pioneering brain surgeries kept her very busy (she was a nurse in A & E), and Dad wasn't around because he lived in a lighthouse (he'd moved out a year ago to a flat above a photocopying shop in Birmingham).

When the storm woke him in the night, Ty had a shiny *new* fib to tell. He'd run between Mum and

Kiki's bedrooms, yelling that he'd seen tiny neon-yellow spaceships zigzagging across the blackened sky.

And now here he was, on national TV, blabbing his spaceship fantasy to the whole country. Kiki and Mum swapped glances, united in weariness at Ty's unstoppable habit of telling tall tales.

"Ha! So there we have it," said the reporter, turning back to face the camera with a wry smile. "Last night's storm and flooding were caused by aliens. It's official! Back to you in the studio, John."

"But it's TRUE!" roared Ty, as a pair of rangy arms – belonging to Eddie – reached in, grabbed the back of the inflatable flamingo and dragged it out of shot.

Lisa stared at the camera and held on to her rigid grin.

The hooded boy stared at the retreating flamingo and its rider.

The screen switched back to the newscaster in the studio.

And Kiki felt her blood run cold.

Please, please, PLEASE let none of my friends have seen that, she thought frantically.

PLING

And *there* it was, the message that mattered most. The one from the Queen of the Popular Crew. Lola.

OMG, Kiki. Is your little bro for real? ALIENS! Own the shame, friend! #hahaha

Whenever school started back, it would be way too soon to live this down.

In that second, Kiki wished a stray spaceship would beam her up and speed her away to *wherever* wasn't here.

ABOUT THE AUTHOR

As a schoolgirl, **Karen McCombie** lived on the fifteenth
floor of a high-rise block in the seaside city of Aberdeen,
Scotland. Gazing out of her bedroom window, she'd daydream
endlessly, making up stories about the people bustling around
in the busy streets below. Sometimes, she'd be treated to the
spectacle of a storm rolling in from the North Sea, the
whole sky filled with buffeting black clouds, and sheets
of lightning glimmering as far as the eye could see.

Many years later, Karen – by now a highly acclaimed children's
author – sat in her house in London, playing around with ideas
for her latest book. Out of nowhere, she vividly recalled the
storms she'd loved to watch as a child. From that spark of a
memory, came the beginning of *How To Be A Human*. And the
character of Stan the Star Boy…? He might have something
in common with the dreamy girl who wondered how
she'd fit into the world when she grew up!

Karen still loves to daydream and to skywatch from
the hill behind her house, but nowadays her
husband, teenager or puppy keep her company.

karenmccombie.com • @KarenMcCombie